A CHILD OF
BLACK
- A Nov
Shamee

Copyright © 2013 by True Glory Publications
Published by True Glory Publications LLC
ISBN-1518649564   ISBN - 9781518649561
First Edition
Email: shameekspeight199@gmail.com
Follow on Twitter: Bless_45
Facebook: Shameek A. Speight

This novel is a work of fiction. Any resemblances to actual events, real people, living or dead, organization, establishments, locales are products of the author's imagination. Other names, characters, places, and incidents are used fictitiously.

Cover design/Graphics: www.mariondesigns.com
Editors: Shawnna Robinson & Jacqui Darns

Acknowledgments:

It has only been the power of God, my Lord and Savior Jesus Christ, that I have been able to persevere through many of the trials I've been dealt in my life. I thank him for giving me the strength to move on.

To my family; my beloved sisters, thank you for believing in me. To my mother, I love you very much. To my aunt, I love you. To my daughter, Niomi, I do all this for you Princess. To Shawnna Robinson, you have been my right hand pushing me along the way and I love you for it, thank you so much. To all the men and women who are locked up, hold your head up and keep your faith; there will be a brighter day. To my niggas in the hood, I told you I could sell books. To Antoine Inch Thomas, thank you for teaching me all about the book game. To all the fans, thank you for all your support. To my Facebook Group, Team True Glory, you're the best, I love every one of you, we're more than a team we're a family.

A CHILD OF A CRACKHEAD IV: BLACK ICE JOURNEY

Chapter 1

Coast Guard Bill Orell looks at his daughter as she sleeps in the hospital bed. Standing next to him was Sergeant Justin.

"I'd like to thank you for bringing my daughter back to me, she is my world. The doctor said she's pregnant with five STD's. She looks so skinny. There's no telling what that monster did to her."

"Don't thank me sir, it was Michael Jr. who found the island that Black Ice was hiding on and he killed him. We found traces of Black Ice's D.N.A. in the explosion." Sergeant Justin replied.

"Do you trust him and believe that he killed that monster, his own father. He could be just like him." Bill replied.

"I trust him, if you saw what his family and loved ones went through you would know he's nothing like his father, and yes I saw Black Ice's head for myself."

"Okay Sergeant Justin I believe you, but just between us, what was the machine that Black Ice stole?" Bill asks.

"Okay I'll share with you but you can never speak of this. The United States government has always feared that we will run out of ways to feed the USA population. So for years we've been cloning animals for meat. The whole world eats cloned meat and doesn't know it. It's perfectly safe but the world doesn't know or is blind to the fact just like the Government wants it to be. The main job of the small military research lab that Black Ice broke into was to experiment on growing and cloning full grown, healthy animals in the matter of a short time. We couldn't have that machine and equipment in the hands of a psychopath, even knowing he only had enough equipment to only make the machine work once." Sergeant Justin said.

"Wow, so what could a psycho like Black Ice do with that?" Bill asks then an idea came to his mind. "Can this machine also clone humans?"

Sergeant Justin stood still in a daze before speaking,

"Yes it can be done, but never has it been done that I know of, and besides, it will take months to pull that off. He probably killed the two scientists he kidnapped a long time ago, and he's dead now." Sergeant Justin stated.

Bill Orell looks at him as a sick feeling comes in his stomach.

Chapter 2

Michael pulls his truck into the garage, and watch as the garage door closes behind him. He turns his head and looks at the black shirt tied up like a gift. A creepy weird feeling bubbles deep in his gut. *'It's finally over, I can live a normal life now with Envy, even with Mike, but why do I feel so bad. I feel like it will never really end, like the rage and hunger of killing will never be satisfied. I want to forget killing Black Ice. He was my father no matter how evil he was. I just got to shake these emotions and bad wishes off,'* Michael thinks to himself.

"Ahhhh, it can't be! Lord no, please no! Not again! The devil I rebuke you!" Rachael screams as she pops out of her sleep and quickly grabs the sawed off chrome shotgun from under her pillow. Sweat drips down her face as she scans her room.

"You know that you belong to me and that no weapon formed by me can stop me Rachael. I'll be coming for you real soon, baby," Rachael heard a voice boom and couldn't tell if she was really hearing it or was it coming from inside her head.

"Get out of my head! Get out of my head, sinister!" she shouts. "Our Father which art in heaven, Hallowed be thy name. Thy kingdom come, Thy will be done in earth, as it is in heaven. Give us this day our daily bread. And forgive us our debts, as we forgive our debtors. And lead us not into temptation, but deliver us from evil: For Thine is the kingdom, and the power, and the glory, forever. In Jesus name I pray, Amen," she reopens her eyes and sees her bedroom once more then looks at the digital clock on the nightstand that read 8:00 a.m.

"I over slept, I never over sleep," she climbs down just a little still grabbing the shotgun tightly, "Michael!" she says out loud and grabs her flip phone to dial his number.

Michael sits in his truck on the grass of his trophy house with his head laid back on the head rest of the driver's seat. He tries to come to a conclusion as to why he is feeling so emotional and why he's having this bad vibe in his stomach. One thing that he learned from Black Ice was to always listen to your instincts. Your body will warn you letting you know that something is wrong way before it happens. It is up to you to listen and react to it. He feels his phone vibrating in his right pocket. He digs in his pocket and pulls out his phone to see a picture of his mother pop up on his screen. He accepts the call, "Hello mother are you okay?" Michael asks.

"No, I'm not okay! I had another bad dream or nightmare," Rachael says.

Michael shakes his head. *'Damn I thought after we killed Black Ice her dreams would stop. At times I wonder if she is losing her damn mind or the crack has eaten away too much of her brain cells. I know being with my father has mentally broken her down and being raped by her uncle hasn't helped her mentally one bit. My mother is the strongest woman I know. Shit it's the only reason I'm attracted to strong women and that's why I'm with Envy, but I question if she still has it all there in her head. At the end of the day, she's still my mother,'*

Michael thinks to himself then sighs before speaking, "Mother your dreams should have stopped by now. I know everything just happened last night and it's still in your head, but it's over now, we're no longer in danger." Michael replies.

"Boy don't you talk to me like I'm crazy. I'm still your mother and carried your ten pound ass for eight months. My dreams are warning signs from God it's not over my child. We're still in danger. The devil is trying to fool us. Your father isn't dead," Rachael replies.

Michael did his best to control his anger as he becomes frustrated, "Mother you were there, you shot him, Envy filled him with holes, Mike caught him with those throwing knives and I chopped off his head.

I have his head with me now." Michael replies.

"That's another thing, when have you started collecting body parts? Why didn't you just leave his head there? Do not become like your father. Have you said your prayers this morning?" Rachael says.

"No mother I didn't and I will never be like him," Michael responds wanting to end the conversation. He loves his mother, but in his eyes she comes off as an insane woman. Everything that came out of her mouth was about God or the devil.

"Boy you know I raised you in the house of the Lord. You must say the Lord's Prayer every day. The devil is real and alive. I don't know how, but Black Ice isn't dead. He is younger and more dangerous than before. I see it clear and he is coming for us and his grandchildren. There are more children out there in this world with his blood and one will kill you Michael if you're not prepared. You don't have to believe me. My dreams come from God," Rachael says with tears pouring down her cheeks. While rocking back and forth on the bed holding the sawed off chrome shotgun like a baby, she's holding the cellphone in her right hand to her ear.

"Mother, you're losing your mind. I don't mean any disrespect, but the dead can't come back alive, it makes no sense. He is dead, we killed him, and so it's over mother. I love you, but I'm done with this conversation. Call me back when you're talking normal," Michael replies and hangs up the phone then looks at his screen to see that his mother was calling back. He shakes his head one more time and stuffs his phone in his pocket then grabs the shirt that is on the passenger seat.

Chapter 3

Michael steps out of the truck and enters the trophy house through a door that's connected to the garage. He walks to the ADT keypad on the wall and punches in the security code. He looks around the house. It is completely empty except for a brown chair that is on the wooden floor that has a light coat of dust on it. He walks to the staircase and heads up the stairs. There are two doors on each side of the long hallway. He walks and enters the second room on his left. Freezing air hits him in the face and body. He studies the room looking at the shelves with glass jars on them. Each jar has a different body part inside of it; they consist of eyeballs in all colors to different women and men's hands and feet. There are also jars with tags on them so that Black Ice could never forget what victim he removed them from. Michael walks up to one of the rows of the shelves and stares at each of the jars. He starts walking to the side as he looks at an arm that had to have belonged to an infant child, no older than a few months.

'Is my mother right? Am I becoming like him? I have filled this room and house over the years, maybe for different reasons, but I still collected parts of my victims like him, but why? Why haven't I just burned this place to the ground?' he says out loud to himself as he walks over to the only table in the room.

The table is covered with different sizes and varieties of knives and other things. There are three inch to twelve inch knives, saws and metal hooks. One of the smaller saws is out of place.

'Hmm, that's not where I left that and it's really too small for Black Ice to use,' Michael is the only other person that knows about the trophy house, *'Unless...,'* Michael said out loud and lines the small saw back in its rightful place next to the others, his mind races, *'I brought Mike here a few months ago. Could he have remembered how to get back here and come on his own? That would explain how he's been feeding the baby hyena for so long without us finding out he had him,'* Michael thinks to himself as he opens a large jar filled with water. Michael then unties a shirt wrapped like a gift, which is holding Black Ice's head. The eyes are wide open and seem to be staring right through him. Michael places his hands on

Black Ice's eye lids to close them then gently caresses his father's face.

'I never wanted this, you did this to yourself. I wish I knew the reason behind your madness. What made you so fucking evil and hate the world? I wish I knew why you despised women so much,' Michael says out loud as he picks up Black Ice's detached head and stuffs it in the large jar and twists the cap on tightly. He walks to one of the shelves in the room and looks at a half dick floating around in a jar with a label on it that read Pooky. *'Maybe my mother is right. Maybe I'm becoming just like him,'* Michael says out loud as he places Black Ice's head on the shelf next to Pooky's dick, then notices something he had never paid attention to before.

More than one jar is labeled with the same name. He looks closely at a decapitated arm in one huge jar then a foot and head. The body parts in these jars look different from the rest of any body parts he has seen in the house. They look grey, like a dried up prune and much older as if they have been in the jar for twenty to thirty years, maybe more.

He reads the name on the jars, *'Sylvia?'* His mind now grows curious as he looks around the large room at the many different shelves. He walks to a shelf on the far right of the room and scans each jar until his eyes stop at the third, top row.

'Sylvia,' he mumbles as he stares at the woman's head. Her facial expression is twisted. Her skin is dried up and sunk into

the bone of her face. Her hair is long floating around in the water.

'So what have you done to piss my father off so badly that he has more than seven of your body parts in jars? He usually only collects one piece of his victims,' Michael thinks to himself. He notices something bulging up under the skin on the bridge of the woman's nose.

He picks up the jar, "Oh shit!" he shouts as he jumps back as soon as he lifts the jar up. A secret panel opens up on the shelf revealing a digital lock. Michael studies the lock.

'Sylvia, I see there's a lot more to you than what meets the eye,' he says as he puts the jar on the table. He unscrews the jar top and sticks his hand into it. The water is cold and gooey and has a terrible odor to it.

Michael sticks his thumb in Sylvia's left eye. The eyeball pops inside her head easily. Michael sticks his finger in her eye socket and digs in between the skin of her face until he feels something that doesn't belong and pulls it out. He removes his hand from the jar. In his hand is an old tube with a red top; a tube that is used to sell crack in. Michael looks at the tube and sees a piece of paper rolled up extremely tight inside of it. He pulls the red top off the tube and pulls out the tiny piece of paper. He unrolls it and on the paper it reads 5, 21, 79. "Hmm I wonder," Michael says out loud to himself as he walks over to the shelf that reveals the digital lock.

He pressed in the numbers from the paper onto the keypad and steps back as the shelf starts to shake. A loud rumbling sound echoes from it. The shelf separates in half, opening up and reveals a small, pitch black room. Michael walks into the room and with his left hand he feels around the wall until his fingers touch a light switch. He turns the light on, *'Wow, how many secrets did my father have? I've been coming here for most of my life and never once did I have a slight clue this room was hiding here.'* Michael thinks as he studies the room.

The only thing inside is a brown desk and a black office chair. He walks deep into the small room and sees a brownish color book on the desk. He picks the book up and blows the dust off of it. His facial expression screws up as he realizes the book cover isn't made out of paper; but human flesh. Right then and there Michael knew that he had to read the book. It was as if it was calling his name. He placed the book back down on the brown desk, exits the small room and grabs the jar with Sylvia's head in it. *'Whatever is in that book I know it involves you miss,'* he *thinks.*

He then grabs the jar with Black Ice's head inside it. He carries both jars into the small secret room and places them on the desk. He pulls the office chair from the desk, sits down and his hand slightly touches the book.

Chapter 4

'Damn, I can't believe this shit is made of real human skin. I wonder whose,' he says out loud to himself. He then opens the book. All the words are written in thick dark ink. The first thing he reads is: ***These are the reasons I am who I am, my son! Welcome to ICE COLD HELL!***

Michael's eyes open up in shock, *'How did he know that I would find this room or book?'* he thinks and then continues to read:

If you are reading this Michael, it can mean a few things; that I am dead, hahaha I find that hard to believe. Or you discovered the secret room on your own. I knew only you would find it. The next

thing it could mean is that you will take my place on my mission wreaking havoc to the world. You may think you're nothing like me son, but you're completely wrong. My blood runs through you, my families blood runs through you. I thought I could once fight it, but was truly wrong. All that it takes is one thing to make you snap and lose control, and once you do, it's impossible to get what is your 'human' side back. I didn't want to be like I am, but once I got a taste of the evil in me, I came to love it and enjoyed it. In this book, all of your questions will be answered. Questions like why you must collect body parts, why you're so skilled at killing without feeling any fear. As you read you will understand.

Michael sits back gets comfortable and begins to read:

My name is Michael Ice Sr. I was born in 1972 in North Carolina in a small town called Brookford. It's a town you won't find on any map and wouldn't want to, because those who enter never leave. It is surrounded by deep woods; there are tall pine trees and to find the town you must drive past a meat factory with the smell of death in the air, then travel deep into the woods and then you will find it. I won't start from the beginning or the end.

I came from a family that believed in polygamy. You're smart so you know what that means, boy. I was sixteen when I escaped.

The more Michael reads the deeper he sinks into the words and soon starts visualizing and feels like he is now in the book.

The Colonel was 6'5", all muscle dark skin with a bald head. He wore black and grey with a gun holster around his shoulder that holds chrome .44 bulldog revolvers. It was told that the Colonel was the father of most of my mother's children in the community except for me and my brother Doc. The rumor was that our father was the devil himself. I highly doubted it at the time, but I was young then and now I know it's true.

"Hold her fucking still!" the Colonel shouted in a thick country accent.

"Ahhhh!" the young, brown skin woman screamed. I watched my brothers hold down her legs.

The Colonel gripped the ax with the wooden handle tightly as he stared at the young woman whose only mistake was getting kidnapped by my family.

"Please no, don't hurt me. Please just let me go," she begged as tears ran down her cheeks. She stared in my eyes as if she was asking me for help.

At first I felt sorry for her, but then I remembered who I am. There was no room for weakness in my family. The weak died first and get fed to the wolves.

The Colonel raised the ax high and came down hard, chopping off the woman's ankle with one chop.

"Ahhhh!" the woman hollered in excruciating pain as she twist and turned to the side doing everything possible to break free of my brothers, but she was over powered.

Her hands were chained to the wall of the barn. We had five barns all together and each served a different purpose. This one was used to have any victim that my family caught slipping or kidnapped from their homes in the middle of the night while they were sleeping. The barn that we were in was huge and had more than 30 women chained to the stalls that were used to keep the horses separated.

"Help me please! Help me!" the young woman screamed, but her eyes now left mine.

"Ice, get over here and chop off her other ankle now!" the Colonel shouted snapping me out of the trance I was in.

"Don't you hear me calling you boy?" the Colonel shouted.

I slowly walked over to him without any emotion on my face. "Here," the Colonel said with his facial expression twisted up as he pushed the ax into my arms. He had a dead left eye and all you could see was the white of his eyeball as it wandered around.

"Now chop her other ankle off so she won't be able to run and we can use her to breed. Do the shit fast before she bleeds to death," the Colonel said through clenched teeth.

I noticed Doc enter the barn from the other side calmly walking up behind the Colonel, staring at me sinisterly. Doc was only a few years older than me. He was twenty years old. He was already as big and as strong as the Colonel. I was working out heavily trying to catch up to their massive body size. I was far from skinny but bigger than my other siblings. I looked at the screaming, helpless woman and could feel all eyes on me especially Doc's and the Colonel. Doc never liked me one bit and I knew he was just waiting for the opportunity to kill me one day.

From day one, it was said that me and Doc were the sons of the devil. It would be our mother who would continue to run the family and make an offspring that would be like no other. She said that the outside world was weak and we were strong and should rule it all. I read every day so that I could get my head on straight realizing that my family was crazy and we were a cult that lived deep in the fucking woods. I knew it was more to the world than North Carolina and killing from the age of five.

The Colonel would hang live pigs upside down and we were forced to stab them. He would say killing and stabbing pigs was the closest thing to human flesh and I had killed a few. See, in my family anyone is allowed to change and kill the other. I had killed five of my older siblings who tested me, but I had yet to kill a woman or any victim my family had snatched up.

"Boy why the hell are you hesitating. If you hesitate you die," the Colonel shouted and back smacked me.

I dropped the ax as my facial expression balled up in anger, twisted to the side from the power of his strike. I straightened my head out and stared dead in his eyes as my hand slowly reached to my side where I kept my rusted, but sharp machete in a holster that was connected to my belt. The Colonel only had one good eye, but seemed to know what I was thinking as his hands gripped the handle of the chrome 44 in his left shoulder holster.

"Go ahead boy! You feeling froggy? Jump if you think that you can take me! Make your move! I don't care if you are the son of the devil, I'll drop you where you stand then chop your little ass up and feed you to the wolves like I do everybody else!" the Colonel said through clenched teeth. He meant every word not taking his one good eye off of me, waiting for my reaction.

'I can take him; he can't be faster than me. I'll chop his fucking hands off before he can even pull out that gun, but now isn't the time or place,' I thought to myself as I remembered the last three of my siblings he killed; his own offspring, when they challenged him.

Even though he was an older man, he was the best killer in our family and the one to teach all of us how to fight, hurt and kill even though my mother said me and Doc never needed training. Killing was already in our blood and will come naturally. I put my rusted machete in the air and swung four times. In a blink of an eye I chopped off his right hand.

"Ahhhh!" The Colonel hollered, but his scream was cut short as the edges of my blade spilt open his neck.

Blood gushed out of his neck and sprayed onto the young, brown skinned woman and my two brothers who were holding her legs. She screamed more in horror as I swung twice more at the Colonel's neck. His neck was thick and full of muscles. I took one last swing with all of my might to cut his head completely off sending it flying in the air and watched it as it hit the floor, rolled and rested upside down. I stood there breathing hard covered in blood with an evil smile on my face.

"So what's it gone be boy, you gone try your luck today or what? Are you finna make your move?" the Colonel said in a deep, country accent that snapped me back into reality. I could see me killing him as clear as day. The image played over and over in my mind, *'What if I wasn't fast enough and he drew that gun and put a bullet in between my eyes?'* I thought to myself as I slowly removed my hand from the handle of my machete.

"Just like I thought, you're soft and not finna do shit!" the Colonel said in his thick, country accent. I stared back into the Colonel's cold eyes and everything in my body wanted to attack.

I flinched as an evil wicked smile spread across Doc's face as he brushed passed the Colonel and removed one of the hatchets from the brown, leather holster on his waist. His eyes had an orange look to them as he swung down causing my other two brothers that were holding the young, brown skin woman to move backwards. The Colonel jumped out of shock mixed with fear as the young woman's face split in half in a weird angle. She didn't even have time to scream as Doc swung again cutting off her head sending blood squirting everywhere. We all stood back and watched the young woman's body twitch around like a fish out of water as blood poured from her neck. Doc stared down at her with a sick look in his eyes, smiling, proud of his work. He turned his head towards me and his facial expression changed to pure hate as if he wished it was me whose head was cut off. I knew it was bad blood between us and one day it was going to be me or him. I stared back without blinking.

"What the fuck was that Doc? I just wanted her foot chopped off so she couldn't run, not her damn face or head you stupid fool!" the Colonel shouted then flinched as Doc turned towards him.

Doc was the only one the Colonel feared next to Sylvia, but did his best not to show it. Any sign of weakness meant death in our family.

"You need to watch your mouth. The only reason I haven't gutted you like a pig yet is because my mother wouldn't let me hear the end of it, but if you value the piece of shit life you have, don't make the mistake of raising your voice at me. You may control everybody else in this family, but not me. So keep that in mind because it's only a matter of time before I'm in control," Doc said through his clenched teeth meaning very word.

Doc walked off and brushed passed the Colonel, bumping his shoulder. The Colonel was in great shape. He always wore a white tank top showing off his arms. He outweighed Doc only by a few pounds. Between the Colonel, me and Doc, we were the strongest and the deadliest in our family. I was smaller than them both, even though I ate like a woman who was eight months pregnant and worked out daily trying to past them.

Anger rose in the Colonel's body. His brown complexion looked as if it was turning bright red as Doc walked past him as if he was an insect; a fly that was buzzing in his ear that he could easily swat. The Colonel stared at Doc's large back as his finger slowly touched the handle of one of his .44 bulldog revolvers.

Doc stood in his tracks and busted out laughing, "Hahaha!" the hatchet he used to chop the young woman's face in half was in his right hand. The blade still had blood on it, "I'm not Ice Colonel, I won't just wait and think about it. There will be no hesitating. So what's it gone be?" Doc said with a deep voice, without even turning around to look at him.

The Colonel kept his hand on the handle of his gun ten seconds longer then released it. "Just like I thought," Doc said through his clinched teeth and continued to walk out of the barn from the other end.

'Pussy ass Colonel, I know this weak man can't be my father. How can he fear Doc anyway?' I thought as a smile spread across my face.

The Colonel turned towards me, "What the fuck are you smirking for? You think shit funny huh? You disobeyed the rules and you know what that mean!" the Colonel shouted with rage in his eyes looking for someone to take his anger out on.

Chapter 5

Next thing I know, two of my oldest brothers rushed me. I grabbed Wade by the arm twisting it around behind his back.

"Ahhhh! Let go, let go!" he screamed in agonizing pain.

I smiled then pushed upwards. The sound of his arm breaking did something to me. It was a feeling that was hard to explain. It was a mixture of maybe joy, excitement and evil deep inside my soul. *'Why am I feeling this way,'* I thought to myself, *'Why does it feel so good to cause others pain?'* I questioned myself. I pushed Wade to the ground and spun and kicked my next brother Mark in the chin then ran up on him and pushed my thumb into his left eye. I rarely cut my nails, if anything I file them to make them sharper knowing I could use them as weapons.

"Ahhhh! Ice let go, let go!" Mark hollered in pain as he swung at my face. Even though he was taller and older than me, I was way stronger.

At times I questioned where I got this strength from. As a child, I learned the more angry that I become the stronger I was.

"Ahhhh! Ice, please stop. We were doing what the Colonel asked, you know the rules!" Mark screamed. I dug my thumb nail deeper into his eye socket until his eye seemed to pop and pieces of it and blood oozed down my hand.

"Ahhhh! Oh shit! Oh Shit! Oh fucking shit!" Mark hollered in excruciating pain as he tried his best to break free of my grip.

The sight of his blood on my hands turned me on and made me yearn for more. Then I felt a hard blow to the back of my head sending me stumbling forward. It caused me to pull my thumb out of Mark's eye socket, as he fell on the floor crying like a newborn baby. I turned around just in time as the Colonel was about to whack me once again with the butt of his gun. As strong as he looks, I'm shocked that the first blow didn't knock me out, but sent me stumbling just a little. I raised my left hand to block his blow and locked his arm between my bicep. In the blink of an eye, I grabbed his windpipe with my right hand and dug my nails in. In my family you never know what will happen.

"Ugah! Ughhh!" the Colonel gasped for air as he looked me in the eyes. My finger nails pierced his skin as I squeezed tighter and watched the blood from his neck drip down onto my hand as he struggled to breathe. A smirk spread across my face. My heart raced at the sight of blood and the smell of fear did something to me. I just can't explain and still don't understand.

I looked the Colonel straight into his eyes, "You thought Doc was the one you had to fear, huh Pops? You were completely wrong. I'm going to enjoy taking your life." I never tried this move on a human before. It worked on a puppy and a cat I once had. I snatched their windpipes out of their throat.

"It's going to be exciting to see how long it's going to take until your lungs fill up with your own blood and you choke on it," I said as I dug my finger nails even deeper and pulled with all of my might.

"Ughhh!" I gasped for air as a razor sharp knife pressed against my Adams apple. I didn't need to know who it was. There was only one person that moved that fast in my family and can catch me off guard. I already knew who it was. The smell of wild berries hit my nose; her favorite shampoo.

"Mom what are you doing?" I asked as she applied more pressure to the blade on my neck.

"I should be asking you the same thing Michael. Release your fucking grip on the Colonel's windpipe now or I'll slit your neck like a fat hog!"

"Yes mother," I replied. I feared no one, not even death, but when it came to my mother Sylvia, fear consumed my body and anyone with common sense would fear her.

The things I've seen her do with my own two eyes could make a grown man cry. I released the Colonel's windpipe and as soon as I did I received two punches to my kidney. "Ughhh!" Then I got one to my chest knocking the air out of me, "Ughhh! Ahhhh!" I coughed and bent over in pain and reached for my rusted machete in the holster on my side.

"Nah ah son, don't you dare!" I heard my mother's voice. For a second I forgot that she still had the blade pressed against my neck.

"You were wrong Michael. What did I tell you about being weak and feeling bad for others? I taught you all my life not to give a fuck about others and kill them fast because if they had the opportunity they would kill you with no hesitation," Sylvia said then removed the blade from my neck.

I grilled down the Colonel with a devilish look. Everything in my body wanted to attack him and rip his fucking head off and piss in his wound. The Colonel's fingers rested on the handle of one of his chrome .44 bulldog revolvers in the holster on his shoulder as if he could read my mind. I gritted me teeth. I was holding in so much and I was so sick and tired of my so called family. There had to be more to this world than what Momma and the Colonel had shown me. I fought through my tears as hate rose, not just for the Colonel, but for everything around me.

Sylvia turned me around and grabbed me by the chin and looked into my eyes, "Boy you are fucking weak? I swear I don't know what the hell I'm going to do with you. Why can't you be more like your older brother Doc? You two are very special, I keep telling you that!" Sylvia shouted while swinging the blade around in her hand as if she wanted to poke me a few times.

To be forty five, Sylvia looked like she was thirty and no way showed any signs of having seventeen children. She had thick thighs, a thin waist and a fat ass. Her face was beautiful, like the face of an angel. You would never know she was a cold blooded killer if you didn't look into her eyes. Her eyes are dark and evil. They say the eyes are the window to the soul. Well look into my mother's eyes and you'll see death, pain and a person that enjoys killing. Doc and I had our mother's eyes, but not our other siblings. We couldn't hide who we were with our eyes. Sylvia was a short woman, no more than 5'2", but her arms were stronger looking than most men from all the pushups she did. She was a honey brown complexion with smooth soft skin. That made me often wonder who me and Docs father really was because all my other siblings had features of my mother and the Colonel. All of them had the same complexion, all but me and Doc.

I was darker than night itself. I used to get teased by my brothers and sisters that when the lights go off I was so black they couldn't see me until I smiled. I was picked on so much that I eventually got tired and smashed one of my brother's head in with a rock repeatedly when I lost control of my anger. It was the first time I did that and I loved the feeling. The rules were simple, show no sign of weakness, cause pain and listen to the Colonel.

"You showing signs of sympathy for that woman there," Sylvia shouted while holding my chin with a tight grip and turning my head to face what was left of her.

Half of her face had slid across the barn floor, her body had stopped twitching and blood soaked into the dirt.

"Fucking come with me now!" Sylvia shouted. I nervously followed her out the barn, watching the hand that she held the knife in and looking at her long grey hair. Her hair came down to the middle of her back and it being silver had nothing to do with her age, it had been grey as long as I can remember, since I was a small child.

We were half way to the next barn. I tried not to think of what she had planned for me. I looked left at the silent woods filled with pine trees around our property. I never knew what expect with my mother, fear consumed my body. Between her and Doc, I knew they would be the ones to really hurt me or kill me. Sylvia leads me to a much smaller barn on the side of our property. I barely came to this side or this barn. The screams and things that took place always freaked me out. Sylvia opened the large double barn doors and walked in. It was dark inside with kerosene lamps all around. I could hear screams and mumbled cries in the barn.

"Help me! Help me please," I could hear a young woman screaming.

Sylvia turned towards me, "Ice!" she said looking me in the eyes.

Everyone called me by my last name, but not my mother, she always called me Michael unless she was upset with me.

"I've been training you from the time you could walk and you just won't listen, hear me boy. The devil is your father and lives inside of you. Embrace it, feed off it and let it give you strength. The world took from me, I was raped at ten years old and most of my life by my father. I prayed every night for God to come save me, but he never did. I even told my Pastor and do you know what he said Ice?" Sylvia shouted while pointing her knife at me.

Of course I know what he said, I have been hearing this same story my whole life from her. I just couldn't find myself to buy into these devil and God talks all the time. It made my head hurt and how in the fuck can the devil be my father. I'm at the age now where I can think for myself and not believe all the things the Colonel and my mother had been teaching us over the years. They kept us from the outside world by home schooling us. The only contact we had with other people was when my family was tracking, hunting and killing. As I walked deeper in the barn, I noticed four women naked with their hands chained up against the wall. They were badly beaten and crying, but seeing my mother they knew not to cry out for her. Then I noticed a huge pig about two hundred pounds hanging upside down by his legs connected to rusty old chains. He wiggled and squirmed making all kinds of grunting sounds. He acted as if he was more scared than I was and the women on the wall. I knew what was coming next.

Momma had all of us do it. She said stabbing a pig and killing it was the closest thing to human flesh and killing people. Once you got use to it, it was easier to kill a person. I walked as Sylvia raised her knife and lightly cut into the pig, not deep, but like tracing a line all around his shin. The pig made a crying, grunting sound in pain. It squirmed and tried to break free. He finally stopped hollering when my mother took the blade of her knife off his skin. She turned around to look at me, staring with an evil look in her eyes. It was the look of an insane woman and a devilish grin spread across her face.

"Now you know what to do, practice makes perfect son, make me proud," Sylvia said in an evil tone.

I walked up to the pig that was still squirming around. It stopped moving as I reached him and looked to be pleading with me. I looked back at my mother who was tapping her feet with her arms folded staring at me with an attitude.

"What's taking you so long? Get it over with boy; it's only a fucking pig. I know you're not about to bitch up over a pig are you?" she said in a thick, country accent.

I let out a deep breath and dug my finger nails deep inside the line my mother cut into the pig's skin and closed my eyes as I began to pull.

The pig made grunting sounds as it cried out in pain. I could hear his thick skin ripping and blood pouring down my hands. Sylvia walked up closer to me and I could feel her eyes on me and her presence right next to me.

Whack! I felt a blow in my face as she jabbed me in the jaw.

"Open your fucking eyes and watch what you're doing. I didn't raise any pussies, do you hear me?" she shouted.

My facial expression balled up in anger. I was taller than her and stronger. I wanted to strike her back out of a quick reaction, but I knew the day I did it would be my last day on earth. Sylvia was cold hearted and killing came easy to her. She had no problem killing me or anyone else in the blink of an eye.

"Go ahead get mad boy and use it, but the day you try me I'll gut you and skin you alive. I brought you in this world and I'll take you out," she stated.

She saw rage on my face and I stared at her as if I wanted to stomp a mud hole in her.

"Go ahead and finish up what you doing boy, now!" she shouted in a deep, country accent.

I wondered how such a pretty woman could be so evil and why in the world would someone get her pregnant and let her have their children. I turned around and took my frustrations out on the swinging pig in front of me. The pig's grunts almost sounded like human screams as I ripped away at the left side of its skin imagining it was Sylvia I was doing this to. I went to his right side and dug my fingers deep into the open cut and pulled away seeing how his once pink body started to turn raw and bloody red. It started to feel good, the more I thought of it being my mother instead. I dropped his skin to the floor and was breathing heavy.

"Now finish it," I heard Sylvia's voice boom.

I pulled out my old, rusted machete from the holster on my side. The four women chained to the barn wall watched in horror, crying and terrified to even scream out as they couldn't believe what was taking place. Here was a mother teaching her son how to kill and wanted him to enjoy it as she did.

"Finish it now!" Sylvia shouted.

I flinched then stabbed the large pig twice. My machete went through his ribs and pierced his lungs.

"Arghhh! Grrrr!" The pig made a weird cry out while continuing to stare at me in the eyes. I raised my machete high and came down.

Whack! Whack! Whack! Was the sound in the barn, mixed with the four women crying as the pigs head came completely off and rolled onto the barns floor. Blood squirted out everywhere as if I shook a bottle of soda then opened it. For some reason it felt good to cause pain and take life from something.

"About fucking time, now the real fun can begin," Sylvia said as she walked towards the four women chained to the wall.

I turned my head and really studied the women for the first time. Two of them were completely dark skin; they looked as sweet as a Hershey chocolate bar. They looked to be in their mid-twenties. Fear was written all over their faces. The third woman had to be no more than 17. She was light skin, but if you really looked at her you would have thought she was white if it wasn't for her big, juicy, pink lips, wide hips and thick legs. I could tell she had a fat juicy butt just by looking at her waist. Her hair was as jet black as the night sky, and looking at her I became aroused and felt my dick growing inch by inch trying to break free of my jeans. Everything changed once I laid eyes on the forth one. It was a feeling of lust mixed with something else I can't explain.

She was the same brown complexion as my mother and her hair was mess, a little nappy and stopped at her shoulders. She had a petite size, C breast and was country thick. She looked at least 160 pounds in all the right places, but that's not what caught me. Her eyes were dark and evil looking like mine and my mothers' and she showed no real fear. She had the most beautiful face I had ever seen.

"What are you doing over there just staring boy? Pull down your pants and get to making me some grandchildren!" Sylvia shouted snapping me out of the daze I was in.

I looked at her as if she lost her mind. These were the things Doc and my other brothers did on the regular, but not me. I didn't want any part of it. Killing pigs and cows was one thing, but all this other shit was too much for me.

Sylvia's facial expression balled up in anger, "If I have to tell you twice to do something again I will kill you where you stand!" she shouted.

While having her long, chrome knife around, I wondered how long I could really last in a physical fight with her as I hesitated pulling down my jeans. I watched my mother walk up to the high, yellow woman first and press the chrome knife to her neck.

"Bitch spread your legs wide and you better not put up a fight or I'll slice you from ear to ear. I'll pull your fucking tongue out through the open womb of your throat and just before you die you'll feel my knife tearing the inside of your stomach up," Sylvia whispers through her clenched teeth. Her body began to tremble. I just wanted to run out the barn and get as far away from my crazy family, but I knew escaping was damn near impossible.

"Michael, get your ass over here now!" she shouted.

No matter how much I didn't like what was taking place my penis was still aroused standing straight up, all ten inches of it and the head was hard as a rock. I removed my shirt and moved in close to spread her legs. Looking into her eyes, I couldn't tell if it was the size of my penis that scared her or the fact that Sylvia still had the knife pressed to her neck. The whole situation felt weird at first, but as I lifted the lower half of her body and spread her legs wide cuffing them in between my biceps so she couldn't move, I pushed my ten inch dick deep inside her dry womb. It slowly became wetter with each stroke. I went deeper and deeper moving around side to side hitting her walls.

Surprisingly the woman's facial expression changed from panic and fear, to pleasure and lust, as she let out loud moans, "Mmmm, ahhhh, damn! Damn your dick feels so good. Yes God yes!" she screamed as Sylvia released her grip moving to the side with a sick grin on her face as if she was proud of me.

"Is this what you want mother!" I shouted out at the top of my lungs without looking at her as I pound away like a mad man.

"Ahhhh! Oh god you're ripping me! You're ripping me, slow down please!" the light skin woman with the pretty lips hollered.

A twisted smile spread across my face as I felt my dick harden even more and grow another inch. What the hell is wrong with me? Why is seeing her in pain turning me on more? Why does this creepy sensation feel so good going through my body? I feel the thickness of my penis stretch and rip her tight hole. The head of my dick crashed into her inner walls. The funny thing is, even though it was causing her pain, her pussy was becoming wetter and wetter and it soon looked as she was enjoying it and trying her best not to, but I could feel her juices drip on my balls and down my thighs as she climaxed.

"Ahhhh, oh God it hurts so bad but feels so good damn ahhhh Lord!" she screamed.

I pulled out to jerk off, shooting cum all over her stomach as she laid there breathing hard. I looked down at her legs in between her thighs to see a smear of thick red blood mixed with cum running down her inner thighs. Then I looked down at my dick that was still rock hard pointing towards her. My facial expression balled up in disgust as I looked at it covered in blood. I quickly grabbed my shirt off the floor and used it to wipe off the blood.

"Why did you pull out boy?" I heard Sylvia scream.

I turned around to see pure rage in her face. I wondered if her face stayed stuck like that. The only time she's not mad is when she's causing harm to someone or one of her children are following her lead.

"I don't know I just did," I said while standing there.

"I never told you to stop Michael? You're done when I say you're done. And don't be pulling out. When you're ready to release your load, do it inside of her. The world is filled with weak people. Children with my blood, our blood won't be weak. I will not fucking allow it. We must stand strong and destroy the weak. Now spread the next ones legs and take her!" Sylvia shouted while using the chrome knife as a pointer, pointing in the direction of the next woman, the one that pulled me in the most because of her aura.

"No, I'm not doing this anymore. I'm done with you and this crazy shit. It's just not right!" I shouted.

Before I knew it, Sylvia punched me in the nose and grabbed my windpipe. With her left hand she somehow managed to grab my ten inch dick placing the knife up under it and applying pressure with her thumb, as if she was about to cut off a carrot with one hand.

"I never want to hear those words come out of your mouth again Michael or ill chop your dick off and stuff it down your throat. You have no idea who the fuck you are Ice. You are the devil and share the same blood as him. I'll kill you before I allow you to be weak. Out of all my children you and Doc are very special to me. You two are my prodigy. Now stick your dick inside her before I chop it off!" Sylvia shouted.

Chapter 6

No matter how much I feared her and tried my best to keep my body from trembling I still managed to mumble the word, no.

"Ughhh!" I gasped for air.

The rage grew in her eyes as she tightened her grip around my windpipe.

"Ahhhh!" Sylvia leaned her head back and screamed in anger.

I could tell that every part of her wanted to kill me right then and there. What she did next completely caught me by surprise. She released her grip off my neck and dick. She turned around to the beautiful, light skin woman who stared her in the eyes fighting back her tears.

"You are a damn monster! You will kill your own child because he doesn't want to be an animal like you," the light skin woman said. She hogged back sucking all the muscles out of her nostrils into her mouth to make spit. She spits all over Sylvia's face and it slowly dripped down her chin.

To my surprise Sylvia just smiled calmly and wiped the spit from her face. What scared me the most was that it was no sign of anger on her face at all. She slowly walked over to the light skin woman and tightly grabbed her by the chin and forced her lips onto hers. The young woman tried to pull away and turn her head as Sylvia kissed her seductively and used her tongue to pry open the young woman's juicy pink lips. I stood there with a puzzled look on my face. Then I see the woman that raised me, the person with the most evil soul that I knew. The young woman tried to scream, but couldn't as she made a funny crying sound.

Blood dripped down the side of her and Sylvia's mouth. The sound of the chains was banging against the barn wall as the light skin woman tried to break her wrist free. My eyes opened in horror as Sylvia pulled her head back inch by inch from the light skin woman's lips. Caught in between Sylvia's teeth was a piece of the young woman's tongue.

"Ahhhh! Help, no, no!" the young woman tried her best to scream out as a huge smile spread across Sylvia's face and chopped down even harder on her tongue.

"Ahhhh!" the other women hollered in terror and shook side to side as if it would help them break free. Sylvia spit out the young woman's tongue onto the dirty floor.

"Bitch, I warned you of what I'll do to you if you speak again. I guess you thought I was a joke, that mommy was soft huh!" Sylvia shouted with her hand still gripped tightly on the young woman's chin. Tears streamed down her cheeks as she coughed up pools of blood trying not to choke on it.

"Ahhhh! No, no, God please help me, help me. Lord I'm sorry," the woman managed to say as she cried hysterically and her once light skin complexion was now red, covered in blood as it dripped out of her mouth and down her breast and stomach.

"God doesn't live here child so there is no reason to call out and pray to him. He won't save you just like he abandoned me in my time of need. There is only one person to pray to and he's not up in no damn sky girl. Besides you're too weak for him to hear your prayers," Sylvia spat out with hate in her eyes.

I watched her facial expression for a moment and I could tell she was no longer with us, that her mind had traveled outside her body and the barn. She was relieving something in her past. Whatever the hell it was, it really pissed her off. The sounds of the young woman crying and coughing up blood snapped her out of the trance she was in.

"God please help me," the young woman cried.

What happened next was so fast that my brain couldn't register it.

"I told you God don't come to this land and won't hear you. What makes you think you're so special that he'll hear your calls?" Sylvia shouted as she swung the razor sharp knife back and forth slicing open her neck. Thick red blood poured out like a river. The woman gasped for air as she choked on her own blood, but that's not what startled me. Sylvia had a huge smile on her face as she reached out her left hand and forced it into the young woman's open wound. The young woman's eyes popped wide open and connected to Sylvia's, then made their way in my direction. I watched as tears filled her eyes and streamed down her face. She twisted and turned struggling to break free of the chains that were holding her hands. She tried kicking at Sylvia using her knees and feet, but her body was weakening from the large amount of blood gushing out of her. Sylvia continued to move her little hand around inside the young woman's throat until she found what she was searching for.

"Got it," Sylvia said in excitement as she yanked until what was left of the young woman's tongue was pulled out through the open wound.

I just stood there in horror as the young woman's tongue now hung out through her throat like a neck tie on a business suit.

The other women screamed, "Ahhhh, oh God, oh God!" they were in terror.

"Shut the hell up!" Sylvia shouted pointing her bloody knife at them.

She then turned back to the light skin woman. I looked at her body and wondered how in the hell could she possibly still be alive as blood poured out of her. From the look in her eyes I can tell the pain was too much for her to bear and she wished for death.

Sylvia smiled while licking her lips. "And you thought God could save you huh?" she said through her clenched teeth. She raised the knife and came down hard piercing through the center of the young woman's chest and pulling the razor sharp blade down slicing straight through to her stomach with ease. The young woman made a suffering sound as her guts and intestines hit the floor. She shook for a second then stopped moving.

'What the hell! Is this what she wants me to be, another version of her psycho ass? I refuse to allow myself to be anything like her or my family, fuck that,' I thought to myself.

"Fucking weak, they're all weak. Their blood isn't as strong as ours baby, none of them deserves to live and walk on this earth, they're pathetic. It will be our family bloodline that causes pain and havoc and someday control everyone beneath us. These were the words spoken to me by our Lord," Sylvia shouted as I looked at her like a mad woman. All my life she sung the same song, the world is against us and all is weak; blah, blah, blah.

'Every day can't be like this, even if this is all I know and have seen,' I thought to myself and wondered when Sylvia would calm down and I could go on my way.

I picked up my jeans and underwear and slid them on both at once then grabbed my black t-shirt off the floor.

"Uh where do you think you're going? We're not through yet and I surely didn't tell you to get dressed. We're still having fun. You must learn all of this, my son. This will come in handy very soon in your life. You and Doc are meant to do great things," Sylvia said with a deranged look in her eyes.

She turned back around, grabbed one of the dark skin woman's faces and squeezed her cheeks holding her face tight. The dark skin woman panicked and squirmed as Sylvia slowly moved the knife around her breast seductively then her facial expression got serious, "Bitch!" Sylvia shouted as she sliced open the dark skin woman's forehead by her hairline.

"Ahhhh!" the dark skin woman screamed in horror.

Sylvia pressed hard with the sharp knife cutting in the woman's face tracing all around it as if she was drawing. When she was done she dropped the knife.

"No, no, ahhhh! Someone please help me! Help me!" the woman cried out hysterically as tears and blood streamed down her face.

Sylvia grinned devilishly and pulled back the skin from the woman's cut forehead.

"Ahhhhhh!" the woman screamed uncontrollably in agony as the skin on her face began to peel off like old chipped paint.

Sylvia smiled as if she was getting some kind of pleasure from watching the woman in excruciating pain. She stopped, turned around and faced me, "See, I started it now you finish it. It's just like skinning the pig alive, but much easier. Human skin is more soft and delicate. Practice time is over my son it's time for the real deal. Feed off the pain of the weak!" Sylvia shouted looking at the woman with half the skin peeled off her face resting on her mouth and chin.

"Ahhhh!" she hollered in pain as her body went into shock.

"Now get your tail over here and peel the rest of her face, finish her off then start on the next one." Sylvia said in a calm tone that sent chills through my spine.

"No mother I won't do it, I don't want to," I said through my teeth.

Even though I feared her I had to stand my ground. Killing people that attacked me or men for fun was one thing, but killing innocent women was going too far.

"Boy I told you not to have any sympathy for the weak. You feel bad for them because they're women. You're going to learn the hard way not to trust women, hahaha!" Sylvia said right before

SHAMEEK A. SPEIGHT

her blade ran across my chest. It split open revealing the white meat and blood as it squirted out onto her face and hand.

"Ahhhhhh!" I continued to scream as I back pedaled holding my open wound with my left hand and reaching for the rusty machete that was in my holster with my right hand. I had a love hate relationship with my mother. Parts of me wanted to kill her and set myself free of her and this world she created and had me trapped in. The other part of me loved her, she was the one that gave me life and taught me how to be strong. If it wasn't for her teaching me, one of my siblings or the Colonel would have killed me. It was Sylvia that taught me how to fight, how to swing a blade. She taught me how to throw a knife, shoot a gun and cook for myself. She taught me how to track people miles away and how to use my anger and rage to make me even stronger. She has shown me so much, but could she have been wrong? I feel in my heart that she is. There is no reasoning with her and the only way to escape is to kill her. Yes I must do it. I pulled out my machete in the blink of an eye and swung aiming for her skull praying I would crack it wide open. To my surprise she dodged it. To be a woman in her mid-forties she moved like a teenager or a black panther, quick, swift and fast, something else she's been trying to teach me.

"Oh there goes the son I know. Let the evil out of you. You want to kill me boy? You got to move faster than that. You're the son of the devil so that makes you him. You should be able to mimic his moves, but no, you haven't paid attention to anything that I taught you boy," Sylvia said.

She wore an evil grin on her face as she side stepped, twisted and dodged every blow. Then I felt a sharp pain on my bicep and my hand as blood came squirting out. She had cut me twice without me even seeing her move. She then kicked me in my intestines, "Ahhhh!" I hollered and bent over in pain.

"I thought you were special, the one to really take over this family. That's why I'm so hard on you. Yes Doc is cold hearted and evil to the core, but he's missing your intelligence. You're a quick thinker, very fast on your feet boy and the hate you carry with you every day for this family is making your soul darker without you even knowing. Yet you're still weak and I'll kill you myself before I allow that to continue!" Sylvia shouted.

"Fuck you! I'd rather be dead than to live this life you chose for me!" I shouted back at her in pain.

"And you shall!" she said as she sent a knee to my chin.

"Ughhh!" I grunted in pain as I fell backwards. Before I could pop back up I received two blows to my temple causing my head to spin. I saw bright yellow stars and a blurry image of Doc standing over me with a devilish smile as he swung once more knocking me unconscious.

Chapter 7

"Hahahaha"

I could hear Sylvia's evil laughter even though I was unable to open my eyes. I felt my body being dragged, no doubt by my sick, twisted brother Doc, because I knew Sylvia couldn't pull me. I could hear the sound of three women crying. *'Damn I wonder what punishment my mother will unleash on me for disobeying her orders and trying to attack her. I pray its death. I'm so tired of living this fucked up life, hurting innocent people for a sport, never knowing if your own sibling is going to stab you in the back and unable to leave these fucking woods,'* I thought to myself as deep darkness was the only thing I could see. I felt my body being lifted up and my hands being cuffed. I'm now hanging there kneeled down. I don't know why mother said the Lord will never hear my prayers, but I don't believe this to be so.

"Ahhhh!" the sensation of new pain made my eyes pop wide open as I hollered. "Ahhhh!" A leather horse whip that had metal tips on it ripped open the flesh of my back peeling it. "Ahhhh!" No matter how hard I tried to hold my screams in I couldn't. "See, you can get away with pissing me off, but not your mother you little chicken shit."

I could hear the Colonel's voice boom from behind me in a deep country accent, even though I couldn't see him. I feel in my stomach that he was smiling and enjoying every moment of it. I could hear the sound of the whip cracking through the air as it hit my back. The small metal tips on the whip got stuck in my skin. The Colonel pulled, ripping a huge piece of my flesh away with it.

"Ughhh, oh God, ahhhh! Fuck you! Fuck you! I hate you all! I swear I will kill every last one of you!" I screamed in excruciating pain as tears streamed down my cheeks.

Whack! Whack! Whack!

"You little piece of shit, I never liked you. You think you're special, you and that damn brother of yours Doc! Sylvia swears y'all are stronger and darker than my children, and that y'all came straight from hell, from the devil himself. You know what I believe? I believe y'all just some piss ants momma's boys. You killed two of my boys today and I'm going to make you suffer for it, bitch!"

I could hear him shouting with each blow of the whip that ripped away at my skin making my back sore and raw. I did my best to hold my cries of pain and not give him the satisfaction and joy that he so badly yearned for. With me not making a sound it only enraged him more.

"Cry out! Cry out in pain. Call for mommy you little chicken shit! Cry! Cry!" the Colonel screamed and swung wildly not only hitting my back, but my shoulders and neck.

With each blow my body became numb. As my anger rose I no longer felt the pain. So I got madder and madder, my facial expression balled up.

"Cry fool! Cry out in pain!" the Colonel shouted.

"Noooo, I will not scream!" I said in a voice so deep I had no idea where it came from and I was unsure if it was even me talking.

My chest was heavy and I was breathing hard. I turned my neck around and looked the Colonel deep into his eyes. Whatever he saw in my face or eyes, made him freeze in his tracks. In mid swing he looked as if he had seen a ghost as I spoke.

"You fucking weak ass man, the first opportunity I get I'm going to cut out your fucking eyes and tie you to the wall then chop your fucking arms off. While you bleed out like a stuffed hog, the last thing you'll hear before I chop your head off and place it in a bag; will be the cries of your weak ass offspring's as I kill them one by one. I'll whisper to you my mother was fucking right, I am the devil in its flesh!"

The Colonel's heart raced and a cold sweat had taken over his body as he continued to stare in my eyes and for the first time in his life he knew true fear. He wiped his forehead to stop the sweat from dripping onto his lips and into his mouth. On his shoulders he kept a leather brown holster with twin .44 chrome bulldog revolvers. He quickly dropped the whip and pulled one out and aimed for my head. His hand shook uncontrollably.

"What! What the fuck are you!" he managed to spit out and I watched the fear on his face as his body trembled.

I had to admit, a weird sensation came over me. Here was a man 6'5", two hundred and fifty pounds of all muscle with his pot belly gut from drinking beers, stood there as if he wanted to run out of the barn. An evil, slick, twisted smile spread across my face as I continued to stare in his eyes. I could literally smell his fear.

"You're not right! Something is wrong with you! You are the damn devil, I'll kill you! I'll kill you!" the Colonel shouted as he slowly squeezed the trigger trying his hardest to keep his hand steady, but he looked as if he had Parkinson's Disease.

I guess he thought I would beg for my life or cry. I bust out laughing, "Hahahaha," my laughter seemed to scare him even more as he back pedaled.

"You are sinister," he mumbled.

Just as he was going to squeeze the trigger, a chrome sharp knife pierced his hand ripping straight through it.

"Ahhhh shit, ughhh!" he groaned in pain as he dropped the gun.

He raised his hand and stared at the knife as blood gushed out of his hand. He took his attention off of it and pulled out his other gun and aimed at me.

"The devil must die," he shouted.

Before he could pull the trigger, Sylvia stepped out of the shadows like a strong, black panther; swift and light on her feet. Before the Colonel or I could register what was taking place she yanked the knife out of his hand and stepped close to him, blocking his view of me. Any chance he had to shoot me was now gone, unless he killed her as well. She stepped closer to him placing the knife under his chin as if she was ready to stab and cut him from his chin up to his skull.

"What the hell do you think you're doing pointing that gun at my son? You're only supposed to be punishing him for disobeying my orders."

The sound of Sylvia's voice seemed to calm the Colonel and make him snap back into reality.

"He's the devil in the flesh we must kill him. We must kill him now!" the Colonel said with his lips trembling in fear.

SHAMEEK A. SPEIGHT

"Shhh, lower the gun, you're not telling me something that I don't already know," Sylvia said in a calm tone that always seemed to send chills up my spine.

My neck began to stiffen up and hurt as I kept it turned around not daring to take my eyes off of them.

"No! You didn't see what I saw or heard in his voice. The voice wasn't his, it was someone else's and his eyes weren't normal. They pierced my soul; it was pure evil in them. I have never seen anything like that, and I've seen it all!" the Colonel shouted.

"Again, I said lower that fucking gun from my son, I won't ask you again. I love you Colonel, you have been loyal to me for years and have given me some wonderful children and if you want to

99

take any of their lives that's up to you, they are your flesh and blood, but him right there," Sylvia said while pointing to me, "He's mine and has a purpose bigger than me and you. He will breed an army of pure killers that will be in my bloodline. I brought him and Doc into this world and I am the only one who can take them out. Am I fucking clear?" Sylvia asked through clenched teeth.

I could see the Colonel's eye balls jump around with a confused look on his face. Sylvia was serious and will jam a knife through his chin and skull. He lowered his gun placing it back into his holster then picked up the next one doing the same.

"Good, now go get Doc and take care of your hand, also push out of your head what you saw and heard tonight, because if not you will always fear him. Michael is like our pet wolves, he feeds off of fear and will attack you because he smells that shit all on you. You're the man of this family and the boys won't respect you if they think you are weak!" Sylvia shouted.

"Yes dear, but that boy ain't right. He's going to be the death of us. You should put a bullet in his head or slit his throat before it's too late. Don't say I didn't warn you baby," the Colonel said in a deep voice and a thick country accent as he looked at me one more time and walked out of the barn holding his hand.

Sylvia waited until he was long gone and wiped the blood that was dripping from her knife onto her long, gray dress she was wearing and slowly walked in front of me. She bent down close and studied my face while smiling, "Hmmm, I wish I could have seen what the Colonel saw. So you finally came out and showed your true colors and let the evil out of you, huh boy? I wish I could have seen that sight. See, I know what you really are because I helped create you," Sylvia said while searching for any sign on my face of what had the Colonel so scared.

"So are you ready to have the cuffs removed and do what you're supposed to do, and be what I trained you to be and no more disobeying my orders?" Sylvia asked.

My body was badly beaten and sore. The barn floor was filled with my blood and I was in excruciating pain. The only thing that kept me from feeling it before was the anger and rage for Sylvia and my family. I wanted to mumble yes mother I will obey and follow your orders, but that's not what came out.

"Fuck you, I will not be anything like you," I said and smiled. My head flew back as she punched me in the mouth twice busting my lips open.

"You may hate me, but you will not disrespect me Michael. Watch your mouth or I'll cut your tongue out boy. You keep thinking it's a difference between killing a man or a woman you're going to learn in the worst way that a hard head makes a soft ass. Women are smarter, stronger and manipulators. We're ten steps ahead of you when you're just making the first move. Just take me for example, hahaha!" Sylvia said and lets out an evil laugh that made my stomach hurt.

I turned my head just in time to see Doc's huge frame of a body enter the room and his eyes filled with hate as he stared at me. I never knew why he despised me so much. *'I didn't want to take his place nor run this country ass family in these back woods; he can have it. My ambitions were way larger; I wanted to see the world,'* I thought to myself as Sylvia stood up straight and walked over to Doc.

"Finish beating him and continue to do so until he's ready to follow our rules," she said then tip toed kissing Doc on the cheek.

"My pleasure," Doc replies with a silly ass grin on his face.

"Wait!" I shouted stopping Sylvia in her tracks as she stood at the barns exit.

She turned around and looked at me. I smiled as Doc picked the whip up that the Colonel dropped. They must have both thought I lost my mind from the confused facial expression they had on their face.

"You said you wish you saw what the Colonel saw mother. When that time comes it will be your last day on this earth!" I shouted while spitting out blood from my busted lip.

Sylvia just stood there staring at me then I heard a sound of thunder and could see lightening out of the large barn door. As rain poured down hard she smiled before she spoke. The lightning seemed to make her beautiful grey hair shine more. She was the only woman I've ever seen it on that didn't look her age. She once told me it was from giving birth to me.

"Well Michael, I'm already aware of that. I told you women are ten steps ahead. I know who you are. You're the one that doesn't know," she replied showing off her pearly white teeth and stepped out into the rain and darkness of the night.

"I thought she would never leave little brother."

I heard Docs voice boom. I was in deep thought over Sylvia's last statement as Doc raised his hand high and the whip came crashing down on the center of my back.

"Ughhh!" I groaned in pain refusing to give him the satisfaction of hearing me cry.

Whack! Whack! Whack!

He swung over and over until I couldn't take it anymore. "Ahhhh!" I let out a powerful scream and passed out unconscious from the pain.

Chapter 8

I knew it was her by the gentle touch. I slowly opened my eyes to see I was still in the barn on the west side of the property on my knees and hands cuffed dangling in the air.

"Michael, I told you to stop disobeying mother and do what she asked from you long enough for us to escape. You're so hard headed," Victoria said as tears escaped the corner of her eyes as she dipped a rag in a small bucket of water, kneeled down and gently wiped my back cleaning the blood.

"Sssss," I made a hissing sound from the pain I felt as she touched my back with the wet rag. "I just couldn't Victoria, every time she wants me to kill a female I think, what if it was you someone was out there doing this to," I said with my head hung low and my chin touching my chest.

Victoria was the younger version of my mother. If you look at them side by side you would think they were twins. It's as if my mother had cloned herself, but Victoria was nothing like her. She was the only sister I had. She was fourteen years old, but her mind was years older, because unlike my other siblings she would read more. While Sylvia was teaching us all the time, we would go searching and kidnap unexpected victims. We would go by a gas station and Victoria would search for books. It never mattered what kind it was, she just wanted to learn more about the world.

Then she would hide the books in the woods so mother wouldn't find them. She was the most intelligent of us all, but hides it from everyone.

"Michael you are a fool. I love you to death, but if you don't start killing and following mothers orders, when the day comes for me to escape this place and go to New York I will leave you behind," Victoria stated as she continued to wipe my bruises.

"I tried and tried, it's just too hard and with all this talk about our dreams to go to New York City, we may never escape momma or the damn woods," I replied.

"That may be true with the way you're going brother. You just keep fucking up."

I heard a raspy, deep, country voice boom. I turned my head towards the door to see my second favorite sibling Booker.

"I should have known if Victoria was here you wouldn't be far behind," I stated with half a smile on my face as I flinched through the pain that traveled through my back.

"You already know where little sis go I go, but you should listen to her because she's right Michael. You are moving like a fool and going to ruin your only chance of escaping with us," Booker said in his deep, raspy voice.

Booker was only 15, but smart beyond his age from reading in the woods with Victoria. Booker was taller than me and no way looked his age at 6'5", with a lanky body frame. He was one of the triplets. His older brothers Lester and Ronnie I hated with a passion. They were nothing like Booker, they were more evil and listened to all the bullshit mother feeds them mentally and was ruthless killers that disliked me and Booker for their own reasons. Victoria and Booker weren't just my brother and sister they were my best friends, the only thing I held dear to me in the world.

"Yea, yea, I do what I feel best," I replied.

"You say that until mother chops your head off and place a stick in it for all of us to see," Booker said as he held up a brown paper bag covering his mouth and nose inhaling deeply taking the glue fumes deep into his lungs.

"She won't kill me, I'm her favorite," I replied.

"Well if this is what happens to her favorite, I damn sure don't want to piss her off," Booker responded while inhaling more glue from the brown paper bag.

"You really need to stop thinking like that Michael. You can easily be replaced by Doc if she continues to grow tired of your ways. Doc listens to her and is a coldhearted killer just waiting for the opportunity to kill you and run this family. I don't know what it is Michael, but when I look into his eyes I see deep hate for you. You really need to think before you act," Victoria said as she picked up the needle and thread.

I looked back at her and couldn't help but smile then looked over at

Booker; he had gotten closer and was lying on the floor inhaling glue from the brown paper bag, looking high as a kite.

"Michael your back is cut open really bad. The Colonel and Doc really did a number on you. I'm going to have to stich you up and it's going to be very painful," Victoria said as she stared at the four huge open cuts on my back, they were so deep you could see the white meat as blood continued to drip from them.

"Man you should inhale some of this glue, it will take away all of the pain and have you forget any worries that you have," Booker said with a big grin on his face showing his teeth while lying on the floor looking at me and Victoria.

"Booker I tried that mess once and lost control of who I was and ended up killing a poor little cat in the woods, along with two women mommy made me hurt. I don't like getting high; it brings something out of me. So thanks, but no thanks. I'll bear with the pain," I responded.

"Okay suit yourself. Hell that means more for me," Booker replied and placed the bag over his nose and mouth inhaling deeply looking as if he was floating on cloud nine.

"I really don't understand why he does that, it's only causing him more harm," I said out loud.

"Michael you should be the last person to judge," Victoria said as she threaded the needle. "Stay still," I heard her mumble as I felt the needle piercing through my skin.

"Ouch! Damn!" I grunted.

"Like I was saying Michael, you should be the last one to judge. We all have a way to have our mind escape this place and away from our mother, the Colonel and Doc. Booker is getting high sniffing all the glue he can until he can't think anymore. For me, its reading to myself or reading to you two about the new things we find out about the world that mother isn't teaching us so that we can't be brainwashed like the others. You are the worst Michael. You go into the woods, trap and kill small animals in all kinds of weird ways, because it makes you feel good. So never judge Michael," Victoria said as she continued to stitch me up and has a good point.

"You always seem to be right," I stated.

"No brother, I am always right and you need to get with the program and do as Sylvia says from now on," Victoria stated as she tied a knot when she reached the top of my back.

"That's one down and three to go," she said as she started stitching up the next open cut on my back.

I wanted to scream as the needle went in and out of my skin, "I just can't do what she wants. She wanted me to skin and pull a woman's face off," I replied while making a hissing sound.

"Michael, please save me the bullshit. You do that to animals in your spare time. Do what you have to do so we can escape. I have the map already and money saved that I have been taking from the victims, the Colonel and everyone else had snatched up. All that's next is for me to take some food so that we won't go hungry on our way from these damn woods," Victoria said as she began to stitch up my third cut and I tried my best not to cry out in pain.

I had to realize that she was right and had a good point. *'I do enjoy causing harm to small animals, watching them suffer as I chop their arms and legs off one by one, causing them to squirm around helplessly as they bleed to death. I try my hardest to fight that urge and not find the same joy in doing it to people, but it's so hard when it's so much fun,'* I thought to myself.

"You have a point Victoria," I said.

"I know I do. I'm always right so don't mess this up Michael, I only need one more month and then we're out of here forever. I love you with all my heart, but I will leave you in the blink of an eye," Victoria stated as she finished stitching up my last cut and tied the thread in a knot.

"Leave who in the blink of an eye and go where?"

Victoria, me and Booker knew the voice all too well, it sent chills up our spines. As we all turned our heads towards the barn door we saw Sylvia standing there in a dark purple dress with her chrome knife in her hand with her arms folded. Her long hair seemed to flow like a smooth river.

"Oh, it wasn't anything Mother," Victoria said in a nervous voice.

"Oh it better not be anything, what the fuck you doing out here anyway?" Sylvia shouted with an evil look in her eyes as she stared at Victoria and Booker while they both stood up.

"Momma, we just came out here to fix Michael's wounds so he won't bleed to death," Victoria replied.

Sylvia walked up to her calmly, "To be my only daughter, your mind should be brighter and your heart should be colder," Sylvia said then back slapped her sending Victoria crashing to the floor.

"Did I tell you to tend to his wounds?" Sylvia yelled.

"No Mommy, but if I didn't he would have bled to death," Victoria said as she rubbed her face.

Seeing my mother put her hands on the only person that truly cared for me sent me in rage. "Ahhhh!" I screamed as I pulled and tugged on the chains praying my wrist would break free and I could rip Sylvia's head off.

During the struggle I felt a few of my stiches pop. Sylvia just smiled her evil grin while staring at me.

"Oh you don't like me touching your princess sister huh! That makes you mad!" Sylvia said.

"Good get mad, get in touch with your fucking feelings boy. Anger and pain will make you stronger, learn how to use it, because I know you want to hurt me now, don't you boy? I'm really going to piss you off!" Sylvia screamed as she sent a knee crashing into Victoria's chin.

"Ughhh!" Victoria groaned in pain as she went flying up in the air and crashed back down to the ground. Then Sylvia began her brutal attack, kicking Victoria repeatedly in the face and stomach.

"Mommy stop I'm sorry, I won't do it again," Victoria cried out in pain as she crawled up in a ball doing her best to resist the pain of each blow that she received.

"No one told you to help him. If he followed my orders his ass wouldn't be in the position he's in now, and if his ass would have bled to death it would have been his fault. You wouldn't be getting this ass whooping because you decided to be weak with him," Sylvia said as she bent down sending straight punches to her face and thigh.

"Ahhhh! I'm sorry Mommy I won't be weak, I won't be weak," Victoria cried out in excruciating pain.

"No! Stop! Leave her alone! Beat me, punish me, it's my fault. Leave her alone!" I said with my head turned to the side watching and feeling helpless.

"No! I don't want you now son and besides, I think this hurts you more than any physical pain I can cause you," Sylvia said while smiling looking sick and twisted in the mind as she continued her assault.

"Help her! Help her! She will kill her!" I shouted while looking at Booker standing at the barn door with his eyes watered up. He loves Victoria just as much as I do and seeing her in this much pain was killing us both.

"Fucking help her!" I shouted.

Booker snapped out of the trance he was in, and ran towards Sylvia. Sylvia turned around as she stood up and pointed the chrome knife at Booker stopping him in his track.

"Boy, don't even think about touching me, I'll chop your fucking hands off."

Booker nervously shook for a second knowing that she meant every word. He looked as if the high from sniffing glue has clouded his judgment as he charged Sylvia while screaming a war cry. He was way taller than our mother and stronger, but not faster. Sylvia hiked up her purple dress and jumped up in the air with both feet, drop kicking him before he could register what had taken place. He was lying flat on his ass. Sylvia popped up off the floor and moved almost as fast as a paper cut.

"Ahhhh!" Booker hollered in pain as the sharp knife ripped and tore through the meat of his wrist.

"Hmmm, I must sharpen my knife. I should have been able to cut that off with one slice," she said sarcastically as she realized the knife did cut through his bone.

Booker raised his arm toward his face to see his hand dangling, ripped open and only attach to his body by a cracked, shattered bone. Blood gushed out of it like a water hose. Before he could scream, Sylvia swung once more, completely chopping it off, sending his large hand up in the air, and she caught it as if it was a football. Booker hollered and rolled back and forth on the ground in agony and pain.

"I warned you, now your hand is mine to place in a jar," Sylvia said then looked at Victoria. "Now Victoria you can tend to his wrist. Close it up so it will stop the bleeding, and fucking do it now before his punk ass die over there crying like a weak baby," Sylvia said, as spit flew out her mouth. She wiped the blood off her knife on her purple dress.

Victoria moaned and groaned in pain as she eased off the ground holding her ribcage. I could tell by looking at her that one of her ribs was broken or fractured. She quietly helped Booker sit up; blood from his wrist was pumping out fast.

"Take off your shirt," Victoria ordered. Booker stood up with tears flowing down his cheeks, and could barely move. I watched Victoria help remove his shirt, and wrap it around his wrist to help slow down the bleeding as they both limp out the barn. Sylvia walked in front of me, with the chrome knife in her left hand, and gripping Booker's severed hand in her right hand.

"So you're upset that I fucked up your siblings. I can see it all in your face, that's good. I want you in pain so you can learn to use it my son," Sylvia stated.

"One day you'll regret all that you have created in me," I said through my gritted teeth.

"No, I won't," she replied then smacked me with Bookers severed hand. She then busted out laughing, "Hahahaha, so are you ready to listen or should I send Doc to come back in here to whoop you some more my stubborn son? I really doubt that you can lose more blood or flesh, so are you ready to obey me?" Sylvia asked.

In my heart I knew she was right, in no way could I handle the metal from the whip ripping my skin anymore even if I wanted to say fuck you to her. I knew it meant my death.

"Yes mother, I will listen," I replied with my head down.

"Good boy, you'll soon come to realize there's no point in fighting me. You were born pure evil to make this world feel all the pain I have suffered all my life," Sylvia replied then left the barn while petting Booker's hand as if it was a small kitten.

I could feel hot breath on the back if my neck as someone removed the cuff on my right hand, then my left hand.

"Your mother has no clue of what you really are. She says she does but you are not of this earth. I now know some of the things she says are true even if she really doesn't realize it, but you are the evil in the flesh, the first opportunity I get I'm going to put a bullet in between your eyes."

I heard a voice boom in a nervous tone. My body was weak as I forced myself to stand up and turn around to see the Colonel's hand trembling as he pointed his gun at me. The fear written on his face made me smile. I stepped towards him as he back pedaled.

"Don't you come near me; I don't give a fuck if Sylvia kills me if I put a few holes in you. I have a feeling in my stomach that you will do worse to me. You're just not right," the Colonel said in his deep, country accent. "Sylvia wants you bathed and fed then she wants you to meet her in the barn on the west side of the house," the Colonel stated as he walked out of the barn never taking his eyes off of me.

I looked down to see a plate of food; fried chicken, mashed potatoes and collard greens. It's been three days since my last meal. If it wasn't for Victoria sneaking me bread every now and then while I was chained up, the hunger pain in my stomach alone would have killed me before Doc or the Colonel could by beating me. I wasted no time picking up the plate of food. An hour later I was washed up, dressed in all black with my machete in the holster on my waist. I feel like myself once more. Victoria's voice echoed in my mind, *'Do what you have to do so that we can escape. There is no point in fooling no one, causing pain brings you joy Michael.'*

I stepped into the kerosene lit barn to see Sylvia waiting for me in an all-black, long dress that showed her cleavage. I walked deeper into the barn with a nervous, bubbling feeling in my stomach. I turned my head to the side to see the same three women still chained to the wall. I was surprised to see that the darker one was still alive with still half the skin ripped off her forehead that now hung down to her lips. The once red, raw meat now had scabs on it.

"Practice makes perfect son, you're going to stop being weak when it comes to killing women. They will burn and cross you the most in life. Now get to it and skin that heifer alive or the punishment will be worse than last time," Sylvia said in an evil tone that sent chills through my body and the three women began to sob and cry out loud.

"Nooo, please no, help us!"

"Shut the fuck up! Y'all know what it means to suffer!" Sylvia screamed as she tossed the straight razor at my feet. I hesitated to move and just stared at it.

"Well what the hell are you waiting for? Get to work."

I heard a voice echo through my mind as I bent down and picked up the razor and slowly walked towards them. Without thinking twice about it, I gripped the hanging flesh on her face and pulled with all my might.

"Ahhhh! Stop! Stop!" the woman hollered as my facial expression balled up in anger. A feeling of joy warmed my body as she continued to holler in pain and I snatched all the skin off her face.

The young woman cried and I could only imagine the pain she was in as the tears touched the raw flesh of what use to be her face. I turned towards my mother who had a sick, proud look on her face.

"Well don't just fucking stop, finish it!" Sylvia ordered.

I tossed the face on the ground.

"No please, no more, ahhhh, help me please someone help me!" she screamed as she wiggled and squirmed, trying to break free.

I used the razor to cut deep into her skin, tracing an outline like Sylvia had taught me with the huge pigs. Everything I did felt natural and a woman's cry no longer bothered me, it was like music to my ears. I then noticed that the more pain she was in the more aroused I was getting.

My dick grew harder and harder, ready to bust free out of my jeans as I dug my finger nails in the deep cut I made under her neck and pulled.

"Ahhhh!" she hollered in excruciating pain that echoed through the barn.

A smile appeared on my face as I ripped the skin from her breast, pulling it all the way down her stomach. Her body began to buckle. I stepped back as white foam came out of her mouth. I stared at her with a confused look then looked back at my mother. Reading my facial expression she answered the question before I could even ask.

"She's going through convulsions my dear boy, pretty much choking on her own tongue. The pain was too much for her to bear. When you're torturing someone like this, it's best to have them on some form of drugs where they can still feel the pain, but it will take longer for them to die," Sylvia stated.

I turned my head back in the direction of the young woman to see her body buckle hard one last time then stop. I studied her chest area which was nothing but raw meat and I didn't see her inhale or exhale so I knew she was dead.

"Okay start on the next one now," I heard Sylvia order.

I wanted to have more fun with the next one. As I looked at both women crying, I chose the one with the honey brown skin as my next victim. I liked that she was very thick with a cute face. Her brown eyes were filled with water and fear. I took off my shirt, pulled down my jeans and walked straight up to her. The fear on her face had me horny as hell. I spread her legs and spit on my hand then rubbed it on her pussy lips. She wiggled and squirmed as I spread her legs and cuffed them in between my biceps lifting her up in the air. She had to weigh an easy 140 pounds, but I was in great shape from jogging in the woods every day and doing pushups and sit ups. I had to stay working out with Doc and the Colonel being bigger and stronger than me. I knew it could be a matter of time before they test me and I had to be ready.

"Nooo stop! Please no!" the woman screamed as I pushed my ten inch dick all the way inside her and held it there touching her walls. "Owwww!" she let out a slight moan as I began to stroke in and out of her.

"Shhh... ahhhh shit! Shit!" she moaned with each stroke as I went deeper and her pussy got wetter.

I could feel it tighten up gripping my dick, even with her fearing for her life she was enjoying me inside of her. That's when I realized there was some kind of power I had over women with my dick. The thought of it fed my ego as I grind my hips touching all around her walls.

"Ahhhh, owwww, yes, yes!" she screamed in ecstasy as I long stroked her, pulling my manhood all the way out and pushing it all the way back in.

I stared in her eyes and could tell she wanted to hate me, but the pleasure in her body wouldn't let her.

"Yes son! Yes, this is who you are!" I could hear Sylvia's voice. I almost forgot she was in the barn and the sound of her cheering me on made me nervous. I pulled out of the young woman and walked back over to my clothes. I put on my jeans and pulled out my machete from the holster.

"Wait! Wait! What are you doing? Don't kill her, finish fucking her and give me a got damn grand baby!" Sylvia shouted with spit flying out her mouth.

Her words went to deaf ears as I raised the machete and swung the blade right through her flesh, chopping off her left arm.

"Ahhhh!" the young woman yelled at the top of her lungs as blood squirted out.

I twisted my head to the side just staring at the detached arm hanging from the chain it was cuffed to. It was a beautiful sight.

"What are you doing fool?" I could still hear Sylvia's voice screaming over the woman screaming in pain.

I pray she didn't go into convulsions like the other woman did and die fast. I spun around in a complete circle and bent down low stretching my arm out while gripping the machete tightly and came down on her thick right thigh chopping it completely off. I looked up to see her mouth open wide screaming as tears streamed down her face.

"Ughhh, ahhhh, oh Lord no! Ahhhh! Just kill me, fucking kill me," she screamed while slobbering and coughing up blood.

I felt my dick becoming aroused once more. A smile spread across my face and I now know I was every bit of the monster my mother told me I was through my years of growing up. I finally came to terms with accepting who I was, the devil. I bent down and yanked the machete out of her thick thigh.

"Ahhhh!" she hollered.

I wondered why she didn't pass out yet as I swung with all my might chopping off her left leg. I watched it hit the ground and she had completely stopped screaming. With her left arm and legs chopped off the only thing that kept her from hitting the ground, was her right arm that was chained to the wall.

"Hahahaha!" I laughed very sinisterly then stopped. *'Damn I'm picking up my mother's habits,'* I thought to myself.

I walked over closer to the woman and swung the blade and it got stuck in her neck. I then pulled it out and swung four times until her head hit the ground and rolled a few feet. I was so into what I was doing that I had forgotten about the next young woman.

I stared at her. I couldn't put a finger on it, but there was a connection I had with her. She had an aura about her that I just couldn't understand, as if deep down inside I knew her. Her beauty was breath taking. I shook my head from side to side to break the trance I was in.

Fuck what I was feeling? She had to die and I had to see her headless. I raised my hand high and aimed for the center of her forehead and swung.

"Ughhh!"

I gasped for air in mid swing. My eyes opened wide. I don't know if it's from lack of oxygen or from the fact that Sylvia had moved fast, but I was stuck in disbelief. She now stood in front of me with her left finger buried deep in my neck, squeezing my windpipe and her right hand was held low with the chrome knife resting on my manhood. I didn't know if she was going to pull my windpipe out or stab me to death. Knowing her it could be both at the same time.

"What are you doing?" Sylvia said through gritted teeth.

"I'm being what you want me to be mother. Ain't I making you proud?" I replied while trying not to choke on my own saliva.

"You're acting like an out of control animal and you better not touch this one at all or I'll chop your ass in pieces. Do I make myself clear son?" Sylvia replied staring me dead in the eyes and for the first time I actually believed her.

'She has threatened to kill me many times in my life but this time I felt it in my heart that she was serious, but why? What makes this woman any different from all the other women we kidnapped and tortured? What makes her special? I have

to find out,' I thought to myself as I stared back at my mother then glanced over looking at the young woman. "Yes mother," I managed to spit out.

She released her grip from my windpipe and I could feel the burning sensation from where her nail was deep in my skin. I placed my machete back in the holster on my hip while back pedaling away from my mother, keeping my eyes on her. I bent down and grabbed a handful of hair, picking up my last victims head then grabbed an arm and the next woman's head and slowly walked towards the barn door. I stopped and turned around looking at my mother's beautiful face. I smiled an evil grin.

"You can't take the beast out of the cage mother and expect it to go right back in after a taste of freedom. Remember I am what you created and what you wanted me to be," I said then stepped out the barn.

"No my son, you're becoming who you were born to be, the devil in the flesh," Sylvia replied then laughed.

Chapter 9

Sylvia grabbed the chrome knife under her pillow as she tossed and turned. Sweat covered her body and soaked the sheets. She slept naked trying to beat the southern heat. She dozed off into a deep sleep feeling as if she was falling into a deep, dark black hole. The sound of a baby crying made her jump up from her sleep.

"No, this can't be, I can't be here again," Sylvia mumbled.

She looked at her hands and saw that she was thirteen again and reliving her childhood. She turned her head to see Doc who was only three years old sitting up crying.

"Shhh baby, you're going to make him come in here," Sylvia said.

She picked up Doc and held him in her arms praying she could get him to stop crying. The bright sun shined through the thick curtain brightening up her small room.

"Doc, shhh, please baby be quiet. I know you're hungry and mommy will feed you soon as we sneak down the stairs, but please be quite." Sylvia said then realized it was too late as the room door knob twisted.

The door flew open and there stood a 6'1" dark skin man in his 40's. His facial hair was long and nappy and he had pieces of food stuck in his beard. His pot belly stomach looked as if it led the way as he walked towards her. Her body trembled in fear as she held Doc close to her praying she didn't suffocate him with her breast.

"Let go of the little piss ant of a child. I thought you were going to keep him quiet and not wake me up while I try to sleep!" the man shouted.

The closer he came, the more Sylvia crawled backwards on the bed until her back was touching the backboard and there was nowhere for her to go.

"I tried, I tried to keep him quiet but he's hungry daddy," Sylvia replied quickly more for Docs safety than her own.

"You a fucking lie!" the man screamed as spit flew out of his mouth, onto her forehead and Docs forearm.

Sylvia watched as he pointed his fat, stubby finger at her, his finger nails were yellow and had huge chunks of black dirt under them. Staring at them made Sylvia's facial expression ball up in disgust mixed with fear.

"I don't believe you, you little lying cunt!" he shouted and swung his hand back slapping her.

"Ahhhh!" she hollered in pain. She flew off the bed and landed on her back so that Doc could land on top of her. Doc rolled out of her arm and bust out crying even harder as he sat on the floor with nothing but a diaper on.

"Get your little ass up!" the large man shouted as he grabbed her by the shoulders and lifted her.

She weighs nothing and he tossed her on top of the bed, unbuckled his jeans letting them drop to his ankles and stepped out of them.

"Daddy, no please no! I tried to keep him quiet! No don't!" Sylvia screamed and tried to crawl off the bed. Her father sent two blows, a left and a right one to her ribcage.

"Ughhh! Ahhhh!" the blows were so hard she could barely scream as she tried to breathe, but couldn't.

Before she could catch her breath, she felt huge hands flip her over onto her back, lift up her blue gown and pull down her panties.

"No! Stop!" she managed to spit out, but it was too late.

He was already on top of her with his massive weight forcing himself inside of her.

"Ughhh!" she gasped for air as his fat penis touched her walls and he pumped in and out of her while making grunting sounds.

"I warned your little ass to keep him quiet," he moaned between strokes.

Tears streamed out the corner of her eyes onto the bed sheets. She held in her screams and cries for help knowing that her being in pain only turned him on more and no one would be there to rescue her. She turned her head to see Doc on the floor hollering at the top of his lungs watching his mother being raped.

"Shhhh!" Sylvia said while keeping her eyes locked on him.

A half hour later, her father kissed her on the lips after releasing inside of her and eased off her. Everything about him disgusted her, his stank breath and fat, beer belly.

"You gone listen to me one way or another," he said while smiling, showing off his yellow stained teeth that he got from chewing tobacco.

Sylvia watched him leave the room and quickly got dressed doing her best to stay strong as she scooped Doc up in her arms.

"Shhhh, mommy is okay and going to feed you now," she said as she opened the room door.

The smell of food being cooked made her stomach growl. She made her way downstairs and then to the kitchen to see her father sitting at the kitchen table eating. He looked up for a second and smiled showing off his stained teeth and went back to eating as if nothing had happened, as if he didn't just rape her in front of her son.

She stared at her mother as she fixed her plate. She was heavyset and light brown, with short curly hair. Her chubby face turned around and she did her best not to make eye contact and placed the plate of food on the table. Sylvia quickly grabbed it off the table and sat in the corner of the room on the floor sitting Doc next to her. She passed him a larger piece of bacon and watched him devour it as she did her best to eat the overcooked eggs on her plate, but the feeling of her father's eyes staring at her felt as if they were burning a hole in her chest. She looked up to see him licking his dry lips, lusting over her undeveloped breast.

"Schmmp!" Sylvia sucked her teeth as her stomach bubbled up in disgust. She sat up and placed the plate of food between Doc's legs and smiled for a brief second watching him eat. She looked back at her mother and father then went back upstairs to shower and change into her Sunday best, a sunflower dress and made her way back down the stairs.

Her mother looked up from the kitchen table from eating, "And where do you think you're going miss?" she asked.

"It's Sunday momma. I'm headed to church, and I'm already late," Sylvia replied.

"Hahaha!" her father chuckled. "You're off to be a little hoe; you're not fooling anyone. There's nothing but some hot ass boys in church and the (preacher) praise is even worse," her father said.

"You would say that and know if it's true. It takes a hoe to know one," Sylvia mumbled under her breath.

"Wait! What did you say young lady?" her father shouted while slapping his hands on the table. It made a loud thumping sound as he stood up out of his chair.

Sylvia began to tremble in fear as he wobbled his way over to her and raised his hand swinging hard, back slapping her. Sylvia's body twisted sideways as she hit the floor. She looks over at her mother who just watched and turned her head as nothing happened. Tears watered up in her eyes as she fought the pain and shame she was feeling. She eased off the floor and squint her eyes staring at her father with hate.

"Momma, please clean up. Doc, I'll be back as soon as the service is over," Sylvia said.

"Sure baby," her mother replied while acting like she's cleaning.

Sylvia turned around and walked towards the front door.

"Yes, head off to be the little hoe you are. I know when you come home I'm going to smell that pussy and it better not smell like sex or I'll really put a beating on you," he said in a thick country accent.

Once Sylvia opened the door and the fresh air hit her face, tears streamed down her cheeks like a running river. *'God there has to be more to life than this, everything's wrong. Lord, please help free me from my pain,'* she said in prayer as she walked three miles to church.

You could hear singing from the church, *'Yes Jesus loves me. Yes Jesus loves me. For the bible tells me so,'* the sound of people singing as one did something to her and touched her down in her soul. Sylvia walked through the old double doors of the church, and a smile spread across her face as she saw her surroundings. The church was an old house, but seemed to be filled with so much lov. She looked at all the families sitting in different rows.

'I wish I had a family that put me first,' she thought to herself as she found a seat and sat down.

After the chorus stopped singing the preacher stood up. Pastor Willie Edwards had a very strong presence. He stood 6'3" tall, and was stocky as if he used to work out. The stories of his past was that he used to be a big time pimp in Chicago that used heroine and beat people up for fun before he turned his life over to God.

Pastor Willie Edwards was easy to relax around. She smiled at the fact that he always seemed to be preaching straight to her or at least felt that way. It amused her that people in the south always called you by both your first and last name.

"God hadn't brought you this far my children to give up on! You may be going through hard times! You may feel as if you have nothing to live for, but let me tell you something, I have been there myself and walked through the flames of hell. It felt as if the devil was my only friend, but my Lord and Savior has shown me the way and opened up his arms to embrace me as he will do you when friends turn their backs on you. When family turns their back on you, there's one person that will never turn his back on you!" Pastor Willie Edwards shouted and everyone in the church said Amen, while shaking their heads in agreement.

"I'm here to tell you God will always be there in your time of need.

When you return home, read Matthew 7:6," Pastor Willie Edwards said ending the service.

Sylvia continued to sit, watching all the people part the congregation shaking Pastor Willie Edwards hand before they exit the church.

"I need help, it's now or never, if Pastor Willie Edwards can't save me then who can?" Sylvia said out loud to herself as she builds up the courage to stand up and walk down to the pulpit.

Pastor Willie Edwards was straightening up after everyone who had attended service has left. Sylvia nervously stopped when she got up to where Pastor Willie Edwards was cleaning up. His back was facing her.

"Yes young woman, speak," he said in a very deep voice without turning around.

"Ummmm, how did you know I was here?" Sylvia said in shock.

Pastor Willie Edwards turned around and smiled, showing off a set of white teeth. He was massive in size, and his bald head had a polished shine to it.

"Young lady I have been up, I have been down, and it could be thirty people in service and I can tell the one's that really need the Lords help and you're one of them," Pastor Willie Edwards replied.

Sylvia held her head down in shame, "Yes, there's a lot going tremendously wrong in my life and I'm only thirteen," Sylvia replied.

"Come, let's go in my office where you can tell me about it and I'll see how we can fix your issue. My Lord can do anything but fail," Pastor Willie Edwards said as they walked down a narrow hall.

Pastor Willie Edwards and I entered a room that had a heavy brown door. His office was plush with a big red couch, thick red carpet and a huge desk with golden handles on it. He sat on the edge of the desk holding a bible.

"Okay child speak."

Sylvia held her head down, "I don't even know where to start. I'm so ashamed," she replied.

"Start from the beginning child," Pastor Willie Edwards replied.

Sylvia held back her tears, "For over three years now, my father has been raping me." she said barely getting the words out.

"What! Have you told your mother," Pastor Willie Edwards replied in shock and couldn't believe his ears.

"Yes she knows. It's not like she can't hear him beating me. I try to put up a fight, but it came to a point that I don't even fight him no more in fear that he will hurt my son, which he has done before," Sylvia stated.

"Wait! Wait! You have a son, but you're only thirteen," Pastor Willie Edwards replied.

Tears streamed down Sylvia's face and she swiftly wiped them away with the back of her hand, "Yes my son is three. I had him in my bathroom in the tub. He's my father's child and I don't know what to do. I need the Lords help. I don't care what happens to me, but I know by listening to your service that God has to have a plan for me and my child," Sylvia said while talking with her head still down refusing to look up at him.

She gasped for air when she finally looked up hoping Pastor Willie Edwards would somehow help her and Doc, but looking at the situation she was now in she knew it wasn't going to happen. Her body trembled in fear as Pastor Willie Edwards had removed all of his clothing and was standing there butt naked. His black skin seemed to have a shiny glow to it and his penis stood up straight pointing towards her. An evil grin was on his face.

"Wait! Wait! What are you doing?" Sylvia asked as shock and fear consumed her body and she began to tremble.

"Don't get all surprised now. I done dealt with little hoes like you all my life as a pimp. In fact it was a fast ass little heifer like yourself that got me locked up. She told me she was eighteen and I took her state to state, putting her ass to work for me, Hahaha!" Pastor Willie Edwards laughed in a sinister tone, before he started speaking again. "One day her little ass got caught selling her pussy and told the cops everything and even her real age so she wouldn't have to do jail time. So she sold me out and I had to do three hard years. Once free from prison I reinvented myself changing any name to Willie Edwards and I found a new way to get money and pussy, hahaha! I'm still pimping, but it's just in a different way now," Pastor Willie Edwards stated.

"Why! Why are you telling me this?" Sylvia asked with a confused look on her face as she fought back her tears.

"Hahaha!" Pastor Willie Edwards bust out laughing, his laughter was deep and dark, "It's been a long time since I had some young, sweet pussy and I know you're not going to say a damn word!" Pastor Willie Edwards replied and in the blink of an eye, he wrapped his strong hand around her neck and squeezed tightly.

Sylvia gasped for air as she was lifted up off her feet and couldn't believe what was now taking place. She swung her feet back and forth in hopes of kicking him in the nuts, but her struggle was in vein. He lifted her up even higher and ripped off her panties tossing them to the side then forced himself inside of her.

"Ahhhh!" she hollered and screamed, louder than she has ever screamed in her life, as she felt her vagina ripping.

Pastor Willie Edwards was thicker and longer than her father, the only penis she felt in her whole life and became used to. The only reason she cried when her father took her body is because she would feel helpless and weak from being abused by someone who was supposed to love and care for her. This was an entirely new pain she hadn't felt before as Pastor Willie Edwards stroked in and out of her. She reached up and with all her might dug her finger nails deep into the skin on his chest.

"Ahhhh!" he groaned in pain as a sick, twisted smile spread across his face. Yes you little bitch, I love shit like that. Fight back, cause me pain. Go ahead, it only turns me on," Pastor Willie Edwards stated as he thrust in and out of her. Then he punched her in the face.

Sylvia did her best not to scream out in agonizing pain. This excited him so he swung again and again, punching her in her rib cage.

"Ahhhh!" she hollered as tears streamed onto her cheeks then onto the desk.

Pastor Willie Edwards flipped her around with her head laid flat on the desk and penetrated her from the back while making animal sounds with each stroke.

"Ahhhh! Ughhh!" he groaned as he released all inside of her breathing hard.

Sylvia could see a bible on the desk and couldn't help but to stare at it, *'Why God, why,'* she mumbled and was glad the worse of it was finally over and couldn't wait until he pulled out if her.

Little did she know that Pastor Willie Edwards was just getting warmed up; for two hours straight he raped her in every way imaginable while beating her, then sent her home.

Chapter 10

Sylvia sat up in the bath tub trying to let the warm water soothe her body. Every Sunday, for a straight month and a half, out of fear she was forced to attend church. After service Pastor Willie Edwards would take her to his office and rape her. She could feel what was left of her innocent soul fading and nothing but hate and anger was replacing it and eating at her. She sat in the bathtub crying, rocking back and forth.

"Why? Why me? They all hurt me and take advantage of me, even God!" Sylvia screams.

She looks down at her stomach that has grown into the size of a small basketball in a matter of two months.

She grabs her green wash cloth and dips it in the bath tub water, then uses it to scrub in between her legs, trying to wash away the dirt and shame she was feeling. No matter how hard she scrubbed and how hot she made the water, it felt as if she was cooking alive like a pot of chicken stew, but all the hot water and scrubbing made her skin raw and turn bright red.

"Why me, why is the world turning on me," she cried out loud as tears slowly travel down her cheeks.

She reached her hand outside the tub and felt along the floor until she found what she was searching for. She looked at the long metal clothes hanger that she had bent straight and then bent a small hook at the end and spread her legs wide while looking at her raised stomach.

"I refuse to bring another child in this world," she cried as her tears traveled inside her mouth leaving a bitter sweet, salty taste in her mouth, "Ahhhh!" she screamed and gasped for air at the same time lowering the metal clothes hanger up under the water in between her legs forcing it into her vagina.

She cried hysterically as she pushed it further in and could see blood rushing out between her legs turning the water a deep red.

'What are you doing?' she heard a deep voice boom that startled her.

She flinched and looked towards the bathroom door praying it wasn't her father walking in, but the door was locked and no one was there, and besides the voice she just heard was sinisterly deeper and sounded like a came from inside her head.

"I'm losing my dam mind, what's left of it," Sylvia said out loud to herself as she began to push the clothes hanger deeper inside herself.

'I told you to fucking stop bitch!' she heard the voice boom once again stopping her in her tracks.

"God what's happening? Am I going crazy?" she said out loud. "God, God!"

'Don't you dare call out his name!' the voice boomed back.

"Oh hell no, I really done lost my damn mind!" Sylvia said to herself as she pulled the clothes hanger out of her vagina and gasped in pain. "Sssss, ouch!" she looked down and noticed that the bleeding had slowed down confirming she hadn't completed what she started.

'Why would you want to destroy my gift to you child,' the voice in her head replied.

"Who are you and what gift are you talking about? I know you're not talking about this child in me, because it is a curse. I refuse to bring another child into this fucked up world!" Sylvia replied. "Damn, now I'm talking to voices in my head, I really need help and I'm actually waiting on it to respond," Sylvia said out loud while shaking her head from side to side.

'You're not going crazy,' the voice replied.

"If I'm not going crazy, then who are you and why are you in my head?" Sylvia said.

'Hahaha, I'm here to save what's left of your miserable life. It will be a voice in your head, mostly my voice. I'm here to help you, but you can't destroy my gift to you.'

"I must be going crazy, I'm hearing voices," Sylvia said. "Again, who are you, why are in my head?" she asked.

The loud booming voice spoke again, *'I'm the devil, and I'm the one that's going to make you strong; protect you and teach you how to defend yourself.'*

"What do you mean you're here to protect me?" Sylvia asked.

'It was me that let your father touch you all the years. I put those voices in his head. I also put the voice in Willie Edwards head to touch and molest you, to see how strong you'll be. In the book of Job, God let me torture Job, take away his family, take his house, kill his wife, give him a plague and a disease. Yet he was strong in his faith, so I couldn't have his soul. So he let me do the same to you, but you didn't stay strong in your faith, you gave up on God so your soul is mine. My gift to you is the child inside of you,' the voice boomed.

A confused look came on Sylvia's face as she put her hand in the water splashing it from the tub. "I don't understand what you mean, all this time God had turned his on back me. I have no love for God and I have no love for you.

You let my father molest me and the Pastor too. Now I'm pregnant with his child which you're trying to tell me is a gift," Sylvia said, "I must be going crazy."

'You're not going crazy,' the voice boomed. 'I told Willie Edwards to rape you. That's my child inside of you. Your first child is also mine. I have the power to influence anybody by just whispering in their ear and if they're weak they feed into their lust. They feed into the temptation, but now it's time for you to stand strong. It's time for you to fight back. It's time for you to breed children who will be strong minded and kill anybody that's weak, weak like you once were. You're not the same person anymore Sylvia,' the voice boomed.

"What do you mean I'm not the same person anymore?"

'It's time for you to take back your life. It's time for you to listen to me and the voices in your head. It's time for you to start praying to me. I will give you all the gifts you need to succeed in this world. I will provide for you a man who will give you children and help you take over by breeding and killing anyone that's weaker than you. The child inside of you will cause havoc in this world; he will be one of a kind,' the voice boomed.

Sylvia sat there with a lost look on her face. She stood up and noticed that the blood had stopped leaking between her legs, then her lost look turned into a wicked grin. She climbed out of the tub and grabbed a towel, dried herself then threw on a long, white gown. She opened the bathroom door and looked both ways.

She walked downstairs to the kitchen then grabbed a butcher knife, put it behind her back and tucked it in the slit of her gown. She also picked up a steak knife and crept back up the stairs. She went into her room to see her precious little Doc sleeping. She calmly walked over to the bed and shook him, "Baby get up. Get up."

"Mmmm," Doc made a cringing sound.

"Shhhh, I need you to watch this. You're not going to be weak so get up. I need you to be strong," she said to Doc as she scooped him up in her arms.

She carried him out of the room and walked down the hallway to her parent's room then slowly opened the door. The sound of her father's snoring echoed through the room as if he was breathing with his mouth wide open. She walked closer and the creak in the floor disturbed her father causing him to wake up for a second and the snoring stopped, but as he turned in his sleep it continued. She walked closer until she was standing over her father as he slept on his back in a dirty tank top. She stared at his nappy hair in an afro and his nappy beard. Then she stared at her mother sleeping restlessly with her head under the cover.

"Motherfuckers, all these years y'all did this to me, all these years."

'Do it Sylvia. Do it,' the voice boomed in her head.

She raised the knife high and came crashing down in his chest.

"Uhhhh! Uhhhh!" her father woke up in pain. Before he could defend himself, Sylvia raised the knife and stabbed him three more times in his chest. "Uhhhh!" then she stabbed him four more times, "Uhhhh!" Blood leaked out faster than water from a water hose.

"Ahhhh!" he raised his hand to block her blow. The knife went through his hand and into his shoulder blade. "Ahhhh!" he hollered in pain.

"You motherfucker... Every night! I'm your daughter, your own flesh and blood. How could you! How could you!"

"Uhhhh! Stop, I'm your father! I'm your father! What are you doing?" he groaned in pain as she pulled the knife out of his hand and shoulder.

She looked at his pot belly and came down with all her might into his stomach and pulled the knife down his flesh towards his dick, ripping his stomach open. His guts came pouring out sideways onto the bed. She pulled down his boxers and in one swift move she chopped off his dick and balls then dropped the knife.

"Ahhhh! Ugghh!" he choked and groaned in pain.

She grabbed his dick and balls and stuffed them in his mouth. "Ugghh! Ugghh!" he choked and stared in her eyes until he finally stopped and died.

"Die fucker die," she mumbled.

Her mother hollered, "Ahhhhhh! What's going on?" she hopped out the bed and ran to a corner, holding her arms around her body. "What are you doing? You killed your father! Are you crazy? Are you out of your mind?"

Sylvia carefully placed Doc down on the bed where her mother was lying and to her surprise Doc wasn't scared or crying. He had a twisted, evil smile on his face clapping his hands.

"Yes mommy, yes!" he said.

Sylvia looked at him with a strange look then walked over to her mother.

"What are you doing?"

"All these years you knew what he was doing to me, you knew it! Since I was a young girl he's been molesting and raping me and you knew! I know you heard the screams, I know it! You helped me have this baby in the bathtub. You know I never went anywhere so you knew it was his child! How could you just stand by and let him do this to your own daughter, how?" Sylvia screamed trying to understand her mother's motives.

"I couldn't help it Sylvia, I couldn't. I love you, but he used to beat me real bad just like he beat you and it stopped when...," her mother hesitated, "when he started coming in your room."

"So you traded your pain for mine? You gave up and let him do whatever to me so that you wouldn't be in pain? I'm your child, how could you bitch?" Sylvia screamed. She charged her with the knife stabbing her repeatedly in the face, chest and thighs. "You fucking bitch, I hate you!" Sylvia blacked out while swinging the knife, stabbing her mother all over her body.

Her mother's body went into convulsions, falling over to the floor, and then she went limp. Sylvia stepped back covered in blood and breathing hard.

"What the fuck have I done? What did I do?"

'You did what was needed to be done to be strong. I will guide you and after you kill your next victim you will hide in the woods where no one will ever find you, but there will be a guy waiting for you. The Colonel, which will be your husband and together you two will breed an army. Follow my lead, never be weak,' the voice replied.

Sylvia turned around and grabbed Doc up into her arms. She carried him into town and went inside the church. It was midnight, but she knew Pastor Willie

Edwards was up. He lived there and had a bed upstairs where he took her when he would rape her. She walked inside the church door that was always open and went into the back then upstairs to his room. She knocked on the door, but got no response. She could hear moaning from the other side of the door. She placed Doc down on the floor and slowly opened the door to his bedroom that she hated so much. It was gloomy, dark and gray with a small, twin size bed and a dresser with a large cross hanging from it that she despised because she was forced to look at each time he fucked her from behind.

As she walked further into the room adjusting her eyes to the candle light, she could see what looked like the baker's wife on her knees crying as she was giving Pastor Willie Edwards head.

He moaned, "Mmmm, yesss."

His size was massive, so she knew she had to sneak up on him. His back was turned sideways. She ran to the side and jumped on it.

"Ahhhh! What the fuck? What's going on?" he screamed.

Sylvia immediately stabbed him in the back repeatedly while holding on like a spider monkey. Refusing to let go, she then stabbed him in the stomach and chest. He tried to swing her off of him and eventually he flipped his body over and flipped her over on the floor.

"You bitch, what are you doing?" the baker's wife screamed, "Ahhhh!"

While Sylvia lay on the floor, she swung up, slicing right into her neck. Blood poured onto the floor into a giant puddle and she died instantly.

"You bitch! I'll kill you!" Pastor Willie Edwards yelled as he held his wound on his chest.

Sylvia laughed and while still lying down she raised the knife and stabbed him in his balls and in his dick.

"Ahhhh!"

The knife got jammed and she was unable to pull it out.

"Ahhhh! You bitch!"

She removed the other knife from the back of her gown and smiled, watching him as he tried to remove the knife from his dick and balls.

"So you listened to the voice in your head? This is why you're weak," Sylvia said then jumped up.

"Fuck you! What you know about being weak? What you know about listening to the devil? Yes I listen to him! We all do, everybody does! It's the temptation, who can fight it?"

Sylvia screamed as she came down in his balled head stabbing him through his skull. He opened his mouth to scream, but the knife was stuck there. She removed the knife and stabbed him in the chest.

"You bastard!"

To her surprise he was still alive. She took the knife and went straight across his neck, slicing it from ear to ear and watched his body fall.

'Get the money out of the safe,' she heard the voice in her head.

She opened the closet and found the safe. It was where he put all the money from the congregation's tithes. She knew the safe's password because she watched him unlock it many times after he raped her and thought she was asleep. She grabbed all of the money and put it in a bag and ran out the room and grabbed Doc.

'You did good mommy," Doc whispered.

She was shocked for the second time realizing her son was not what she thought he was, but something else; something greater, something darker. She ran downstairs and out the church, heading deep into the woods, where she hoped to never be found.

"Ahhhh!" Sylvia woke up out of her sleep and stabbed the Colonel in the leg.

"Sylvia what are you doing? It's a dream! It's a dream!"

"Hmmmfff! Hmmmfff!" Sylvia breathed hard before realizing she was back into reality. She was now a much stronger woman and now she will feed off the weak and never become one of them again.

She looked at the Colonel's leg. "Stop hollering like a little baby," she said as she pulled the knife out.

"Ughhh!" he groaned.

"Come on," she said and grabbed a kerosene lamp and a bucket of water to clean his womb. I'm sorry," she said.

"What the hell were you dreaming about?" he yelled.

"I was dreaming about the day I ran in the woods and met you," she replied.

"That's the second time Sylvia."

"I know, that means something is about to go down. Something is going to happen," she said.

Chapter 11

It was three in the he morning. I could hear the birds chirping. I stood outside in the beginning of the woods that surrounded our property. I had been jogging and practicing fighting to help release the anger I felt deep inside of me. It did little to help; it was a hunger situation that could only be eased when I inflicted pain on others.

'I must fight this yearning,' I said out loud to myself as my body dripped in sweat. I looked down at my biceps and my six-pack and grinned. I wasn't as big as Doc or the Colonel, but I will so surpass them. While they sleep I train with little rest in the dark woods. For some reason I felt one with the darkness. I was never afraid of it, if anything I embraced it. It's as if I had always belonged in the dark or maybe it could have been the fact that my skin is so dark. I figured no one could see me at night, no matter how hard they tried.

I walked towards the barn on the east side of the property tightening my grip on the machete in my right hand. I bust open the barn door and crept all the way in. I stopped in front of her. Her caramel skin and firm, thick body was beautiful even when she was asleep. I gently shook her face and startled her as she woke and tried to break free from the chains that kept her pinned to the wall.

"Shhhh," I said while placing my finger on my lips.

"What? What you want?" she said in a weak voice.

Her lips were dry and had white crust on the side of them. I could tell she was dehydrated so I walked to the corner of the barn where there was a bucket of water and beside it was a ladle. I used it to scoop water into a tin cup and made my way back to her. I pressed the cup against her lips, she hesitated on drinking it, but her thirst took over and I watched her slurp the water down in a matter of seconds. When I took the cup away I noticed a soft yet hard look in her eyes. She kind of reminded me of Sylvia in a way. How sick is that to be attracted to a woman that reminded me of my twisted, fucked up mother.

"More please," the woman muttered.

I quickly ran over to the bucket and ladle and scooped up some water into the cup and returned. She drank the cup of water faster than the last time, and gasp for air when I removed the cup from her lips.

"So why are you being nice to me all of a sudden? Just a few hours ago you had a dead, deranged look in your eyes and wanted to chop me into pieces like you did my friend. Why the sudden change of heart?" she asked looking at him suspiciously.

I turned my head away from her. The more I stared at her, the more dangerous I felt myself becoming, "I'm not like my mother or the rest of my family," I mumbled.

'Well you sure the hell fooled me. It's like all of y'all are nuts," the woman replied.

"It's easy for you to judge us, but you have no idea what true pain is. My mother has no problem teaching you that lesson. She would do things that would have you wishing for your own death. So yes, you would do well to listen to any and everything she tells you. I know my hard headed ass is off and in a way it's funny. I don't like killing people, but it takes away the deep hunger and pain, causing me to become lost in myself. I'm actually scared that I will become the monster my mother told me I was bred from," I stated.

I could feel the woman's eyes staring at me as if she was looking right through me.

"So why won't you just leave? Just escape," she said finally opening her juicy lips.

"Hahaha!" I bust out laughing. "It's easier said than done woman. My mother owns six wolves that she feeds victims body parts, and all the members of my family are hunters and will take you or anyone else down. We are deep in the woods, miles and miles away from any roads. So like I said, it's easier said than done," I replied.

"It sounds like you're just scared...," before she could finish what she was saying my huge hand was wrapped around her soft neck, squeezing tightly.

"You can kill me if you want, but you know what I said is true," she managed to say.

As she gasped for air, spit was flying out her mouth. I was causing her pain and it turned me on even more. Her comment was a stab at my pride and she had pissed me off a great deal. I pulled down my jeans and allow my ten inch dick to break free. I spread her legs and let my hands run across her fat, pussy lips. To my surprise, my hand was soaked in her sweet juices. She was so wet that it was dripping down her inner thighs. I looked at her face to see a mixture of pain and lust. I grabbed my dick and rubbed it on her clit, up and down, very slow.

"Sssss mmmm!" she let out a soft moan, while still gasping for air. "Put it in," she said, shocking me.

I stood with a confused facial expression, but the hard throbbing veins in my dick didn't let me stay in shock for long as it was best to ease and release such tension. I pushed my thick, long dick inside her warm, wet box.

"Ahhhh, mmmm, mmmm," she moaned.

I worked it in and out of her with short strokes teasing her, not giving her the dick fully. Knowing this was driving her insane, I allowed her to release all over my chocolate dick, back to back. I looked down and stared at the white cum that covered me. I then began giving her long, deep strokes. I removed my hand from her neck and grabbed her hips, thrusting in harder and faster.

"Ahhhh, mmmm, oowee, sssss, yes, yes!" she screamed while winding her hips with mine. I matched her rhythm.

"Ughhh!" I groaned as I forcefully pound away.

The sweet sensation of her walls was driving me crazy and by the look on her face, I knew I was doing more than a little something right.

"Yes! I'm cumin, I'm cumin!" she screamed and I felt her body tense up. She shook out of control and I felt her juices running down my legs.

I grit my teeth as I pump with all my might feeling my dick pounding into her, "Damn, damn, damn!" I shouted as I bust the hugest nut that I had ever had in my whole life all inside her. I pulled out of her, out of breath and looked at her strangely.

"Why you looking at me like that?" she asked.

"Because you have the best pussy I've ever had in my short life. I came in here tonight to find out what makes you so special to Sylvia and why she don't want you dead, but now I'm even more confused because I found out what makes you special to me," I said nicely.

"I don't know why your psycho mother wants me to live, but I know I'm going to die sooner or later. Your dick feels so damn good inside of me. I might as well die busting off good nuts, it's the only way to go. By the way, my name is Javasia. Now come back over here and choke me again and put your dick back inside of me, it's amazing," Javasia said. I grin as I choked her and slid my thick, long dick back inside her.

For seven long weeks, I worked out deep in the woods, conditioning my body. When I knew my family members was asleep, I would sneak to the barn and have amazing sex and multiple orgasms with Javasia, to the point where we began to trust each other and talk about crazy things. I would also remove the handcuffs.

"If Sylvia finds out we're both be dead," I said as she climbed in my arms.

"Not for nothing, but you have no reason to be scared of your mother," Javasia replied.

I let out a sigh, "You have no idea what my mother is truly capable of," I replied.

"That's the same way I feel about you, you're stronger than you know and have a dark side to you worse than all your family members. I say it's time to release it," Javasia replied.

"You're crazy, we're about to run away for good and this place will be just a bad nightmare, nothing more," I replied.

"You are a fool if you think this is just a problem that we can run from. No matter how badly I want to escape I'm having doubts that it can be done. Like really, how far do you think I can run?" Javasia said, as she looked down at her fast, growing stomach.

"Don't worry, my sister Victoria has a smart escape all mapped out for tomorrow night," I replied, knowing in my heart that I wouldn't let nothing happen to Victoria or Javasia and my unborn child.

I pulled Javasia closer and our lips met as we kissed deeply and passionately. "I love you," I mumbled.

"I love you too," she replied.

I turned her on her back and spread her legs sliding my thick, long dick into her soaking wet pussy. She let out small moans with each stroke and her nails dug deep into my back. An hour later I handcuffed her back to the barn wall and stepped out the barns huge doors. This will be the last night; we have

to set the trap. I felt the presence of someone watching us.

'Damn I pray Sylvia hadn't caught me. This will ruin all of our plans. I will have to act sooner,' **I said to myself.**

Chapter 12

It felt as if someone was about to attack me from behind. I pulled out my old trusty, rusty machete and swung backwards.

A loud clanking sound echoed through the night air as metal clashed against each other. I turned around to see that I was facing Doc who had blocked my blow with his hatchet.

"You're still too slow little brother," Doc said as he stared at me with hate in his eyes.

"I'm fast enough and soon I'll be fast enough to kill you," I replied.

Doc just smiled with an evil grin, "Sure you are, but just know that I'll have my day little brother. One day I'll get rid of you. I hate you with every part of my body," Doc said while staring deep into my eyes.

I shook my head, pulled my machete away, put it back into the holster and walked back to the middle of the woods where I felt most comfortable at. Doc stood there for a while watching me disappear then he turned around and head for the barn.

'What is he doing out here so late?' Doc thought to himself. He opened the barn door and walked in lighting a kerosene lamp to brighten the barn up. He walked deeper in and could see Javasia sleeping with her hands cuffed to the wall and her head leaning down. He looked down at her stomach to see the

bulge sticking out. The sound of him walking startled her.

"Ice, is that you?" she asked as she opened her eyes.

Doc grinned, "Hmmm so you're what my brother has been up to. Mmm, Sylvia and Ice told me not to come in here and that you can't be touched. You're so important and so special; no one should touch you or kill you. If it was up to me I'd slice your throat right now, but I think my brother has a soft spot for you," Doc said with a twisted look on his face.

"What are you talking about? Yes, your mother said not to touch me, so don't you dare," Javasia screamed at him.

Doc smiled, unbuckled his pants, dropped them down to the floor and stepped out of them while removing his shirt.

"No, no!" Javasia said while looking at his hard penis that was pointed straight at her. "What are you doing? No don't you dare!"

She struggled on the wall hoping she could break free but knew she was trapped. Doc just walked up to her slowly as he spit in his hand and rubbed it on the tip of his dick. He spread her legs wide and slid straight into her hard, forcing himself deep inside.

"Stop, stop!" Javasia screamed as he pumped in and out.

"Yeah, so this is what my brother be loving? Yeah, this is what he likes, huh? He likes this pussy right here, huh? Yeah I'm gone fuck the shit out of you,"

Doc screamed as he pounded deeper inside of her giving her long thrusts and strokes each causing her more pain.

Javasia screamed and cried hysterically as he pounds away, "Stop! Sylvia will find out, I'll tell her!"

"You better not tell her shit, bitch!" Doc said as he grabbed her windpipe like he wanted to pull it out, "If you mention this to them, I swear I'll do worse than anyone can ever do to you. I'll chop every part of your body off and drag your ass in the woods and let you die slowly as I fuck you some more, do you understand me?" Doc screamed.

Javasia got quiet and shook her head up and down as he continued to pound away.

"Ohhh yes, oh shit," Doc got agitated because she stopped making sounds, but he continued working in and out of her until he released inside of her, "Ahhhh, your pussy is so fucking sweet. Now I know why my brother comes back and forth in here. Remember, don't you tell anybody, I ain't done with your ass yet," Doc said as he kissed her on the lips then put back on his clothes. "I'll see you soon bitch," he said as he blew out the kerosene light and walked back out the barn.

Chapter 13

I woke up early in the morning knowing it was now or never, that we had to do this. Victoria stood on my right side and Booker on my left. We had all our bags packed including everything of value that we needed. I slowly crept into the barn where Javasia was and unlocked her chains.

"Shhh."

She was scared and startled more than normal. I didn't understand why, but I could see the fear in her eyes, "Shhh, we're going to leave right now. There will be no more fear, we're out of here, I whispered. Then kissed her on the lips and I could see tears streaming down her face.

"What's wrong? Ain't this what you wanted for us, to get away?" Ice asked.

"Yes, I believe in you," Javasia said.

"Man y'all talk too much let's go!" Victoria said.

I looked at my younger sister; she is so wise to the ways of the world. I loved her more than life itself and I knew she was right, it's time for us to go. I quickly found some clothes for Javasia to put on and we all eased out the barn sneaking into the woods.

Victoria pulled out a map, "If we keep going south we'll get to this highway that leads to the closest town, then we could jump on the bus. I saved enough money so we can afford the tickets and still have money for food," she said.

"You have it all mapped out don't you sis?" I replied.

"Yes. So where are we going?"

"We're going to New York. It's millions of people there and we can start our life over and our family will never find us," Ice answered.

"Sounds like a plan to me. What do you think?" I asked Javasia.

She shook her head up and down and I still could sense something wasn't right with her. We got deeper into the woods and had at least two days until we reached the highway, so we traveled nonstop with no rest or sleep for the first two days.

It was only a matter of time before Sylvia found out and was on our trail. Our whole family is hunters and trackers so I tried to cover all our tracks and footprints the best way I could. I lit a small campfire so that I could cook the rabbit I caught earlier today. I let it roast slowly and stared at Javasia and her stomach wondering how was I going to support them in this new world. I looked at Victoria who seemed so confidant in her plan, and then I looked at my brother with his hand missing, but still looking as strong as ever. I hope this plan works. I could hear noises in the woods, footsteps and wolves howling.

"We gotta go, we gotta go now! Put out the fire, we gotta go!" I shouted.

"For what?" Javasia said.

"They're on us!"

"It's just wolves," Javasia said.

"My mother has wolves that she uses for hunting. Doc and the Colonel would use them too but they'll turn on anybody. We gotta go that's them in the woods, they're getting close," I said.

I tried to slow down my heart knowing that it all could be over in a matter of seconds. I put out the fire and packed our things quickly then grabbed Victoria and Javasia's hands and we began to run. I could hear footsteps coming up behind us, not just wolves but humans and laughter. I could hear Docs voice. They were closing in on us and we were only a day away from freedom. It can't happen like this.

"Keep running, keep running!" I screamed to them as I hide behind a tree.

One of the Colonel's children came and without me even trying, I chopped off his head and it went flying into the air. I took off running using the night sky as cover. I could hear more of the Colonel's children coming and wolves. The wolves were catching up to the others fast. A wolf jumped on Booker's back biting into the back of his neck and I could hear him scream.

"Ahhhh!" Booker shook his body to try to get it off but it didn't work. Victoria hit the wolf.

"No Victoria, run!" I called out to her and Javasia, "Keep moving, keep moving!"

I stabbed the wolf once in the ribs. The wolf hollered in pain and fell off. I looked over at Booker with his neck chewed open blood gushing everywhere.

"Help me," Booker struggled to say.

I tried to hold back tears knowing it was no saving him. I backed away from Booker.

"Help me Ice, help me please!"

"I can't!"

"Kill me!"

"I can't," I said as I disappeared in the dark keeping my eyes on him.

Two wolves came and dragged his body into the dark by his ankles.

"Ahhh, help me!" he screamed.

His screams soon turned into cries and moments later there was complete silence. I continued to run, catching up with Victoria and Javasia. They weren't hard to find because they were breathing loud and hard. A hatchet went flying past my head and slammed into Victoria's back.

"Ughhh," she fell forward.

"No!" I screamed as I looked at the hatchet in my sister's back. Tears fell down my cheeks as I watched her slowly die, knowing that there was no way I could save her.

"Don't cry, just follow my plan. Do as I say. I buried the money by a tree with a V on it real fast because I knew I wouldn't make it, but you and Javasia can," Victoria mumbled.

I kissed her on the forehead, "Leave me, run Javasia!"

"I can't!"

"Javasia run!" I screamed as my sister died in my arms. All I could think about was how I lost my brother and sister and Javasia and the baby was all I have left and I knew that if I let her run without me she'd be okay, "Go now!"

She ran and disappeared in the dark. As more of my siblings approached me, I slowly laid Victoria's head down and pulled out my machete. Two of my siblings charged me and with one swift move I chopped off both of their arms. I then spun and sliced open their throats.

"You bastards!" I screamed watching them choke on their own blood.

A hatchet flew and caught me in the shoulder. "Fuck!" I knew who the hatchet belonged to; it was the same kind that went in Victoria's back, it was Doc's. I pulled the hatchet out of my shoulder and dropped it on the ground. I didn't know what hurt more, the fact that my shoulder was split open or watching my sister that I loved so much lie on the ground motionless dying right in front of me. I took off into the woods spreading my blood on the trees to throw then off of Javasia's path. I could hear the wolves chasing me. I tripped and fell down a hill tumbling into a cave.

"Uggh, ahhh!" I groaned in pain right before I lost consciousness and passed out.

"Uggh," I groaned in pain and could feel insects crawling all over me. I looked around and it was daytime. There was no telling how long I'd been out. I looked at my arm and could see maggots eating at my wound where the hatchet cut me. I quickly picked them out one by one squashing them with my hands. I weakly stood up and tumbled a little and walked from the cave, up the hill and back into the woods where I came from.

Tears filled my eyes as I saw body parts everywhere. One in particular I could identify by the clothing was my sister Victoria. Looking at the other body parts I could tell I had been out for more than a day or two because there was no flesh, just all bones. I started a fire using two rocks and once the fire grew, I took a stick and put half of it in the fire then placed it on my wound trying not to scream. My heart was full of pain and anger.

"I will kill them all!" I screamed out loud, "But first I need my energy." I kept the fire as low as I could, not knowing if my family was still out looking for me. As the sun went down I could hear the sound of the wolves howling and surrounding me in the dark. I knew it was only four left because I killed one. I could see their eyes deep in the woods on each side of me glowing bright green. There was no more fear in me, no more running, I was tired of it all. The first wolf came out and growled and stared at me as I faced him. He jumped in the air and I sliced his head off with one swift move. Then I pulled his guts from his neck as if I was a black bear, ripping him apart. The other three wolves backed away, crying in fear. I called them to me.

'Come, come.'

They came to me.

'Sit!'

They listened.

'That's when I figured it out, that fear is weakness like my mother said. Now it's time to create a plan,' I thought to myself.

Instead of running to the freeway I went back in the direction of the barn thinking of Doc, my mother and revenge for Victoria and Booker. It took me two days to return home. I could see my family standing in the barn torturing a victim and all I could hear was Sylvia screaming, "Have you found his body yet!"

"No, but he has to be dead, I seen him go down," Doc said.

"He's not fucking dead, bring back his head. That is the only proof I need, that's all I wanna see. It's not over,"

Sylvia shouted then slapped Doc in the face.

"I'm telling you he's dead, he couldn't have survived that," Doc shouted back.

"You're so fucking weak. You're weaker than him. I'm telling you he's not dead, I could feel it. You don't know what you've caused by doing this. You should've taken his head off when you had the chance," she said.

The Colonel there stood quiet. I peeped through a hole in the barn watching him shake in fear. Seven other women were chained up and being molested by my other siblings as Sylvia stood in the middle praying. I went to the empty barn on the other side to grab the canister of kerosene and a rope that was laying there and threw it over my shoulder. I went back to the barn my family was in. I poured kerosene all over it and went back to the woods and found two nice size rocks and the biggest, longest sticks I could find and hand crafted my own spears. I brought them back to the barn where I poured the kerosene and rubbed the rocks together and made and fire. The barn went up in flames in a matter of seconds.

"Ahhhhh!" I could hear everyone screaming as the barn started to collapse. As two of the Colonel's children ran out, I threw the spears into their chest and as another ran out I tossed another spear. It traveled so fast that it went through his mouth and out the back of his head. Finally Doc came out covered in fire. He rolled onto the ground and popped back up. I stood there with my machete ready to face him with no more fear.

"I knew it would come to this. I hate you!" Doc shouted, "My mother always like you best, she always thought you were stronger. I don't know why, you're fucking weak. I hated you from the moment you were born. It's me who will rule this family. Me! Not you!" Doc shouted as he removed both hatchets from the holsters from his waist and charged at me.

I moved swiftly as he swung. He looked at me with a confused look on his face noting that I was faster than he anticipated. I punched him in the face with my left hand then kneed him in the stomach.

"Ugh," he leaned over in pain.

"I am stronger than you and much more evil," I mumbled into his ears.

He tried to attack again, swinging his hatchets left and right. I swooped low and kicked his feet from under him; he fell on his back so I jumped in the air and came down hard in his chest with my machete.

"Ugggh," he groaned. As I pulled it out, he rolled over and jumped back up. "It's going to take more than that you pussy!" Doc screamed, but for the first time I saw fear in his eyes. He was scared of me, he always had been. I can smell it and it turned me on. I threw my machete straight at him, cutting him from his dick to his ass cheeks.

"Ahhhh, ugggh," he hollered in pain.

As he dropped his hatchets to try to remove it, I calmly walked over to him and picked up both hatchets.

"I am stronger, fucker!" I yelled at him.

Then I swung them both at the same time, decapitated him. I smiled with joy. I removed my machete from his dick and turned around just in time to see the Colonel stepping out of the barn on fire. He quickly rolled in the dirt and took out his guns once he saw me. His hands shook as he released the trigger. I dodged the first one and then boom! He fired at me again, hitting me in my leg making a huge hole through it but it didn't stop me from charging at him.

As he continued to fire at me, I chopped off his left hand then his right, then dropped my machete and grabbed his head.

"All the years that you fucking beat me, all the years that you thought you were stronger," I screamed through clinched teeth as I took my fingers and stuck them into his eyes. "You fucking bastard die, die!"

I could feel my thumb going deeper into his eye sockets as I pushed harder and feeling what used to be his eyes turning into goo.

"Die you old bastard. Die." I bent down and bit his nose while my fingers were still in his eyes. I spit out the piece of his nose.

"Ahh!" he screamed.

For the first time I got to see how much of a bitch he was. I wasted no more time and grabbed my machete and sliced his head off. Trapped in the barn, I could hear his children and the women that were still chained screaming for their lives. Sylvia came out rolling on the ground and once the fire was out she too got up.

"I knew you weren't dead, I knew you would be back." I punched her two times with a combo. She fell backwards and got back up like it was nothing. "You can do better than that my son, way better. You're stronger than you know, release it."

I couldn't hear her words, anger had consumed me. She had her shiny, chrome knife in her hands and swung at me left and right trying to cut an x in my chest. I hit her with an uppercut. It was the first time I ever saw my mother stumble so I quickly grabbed the rope and knife and stabbed her repeatedly in the stomach. Then I tied the rope to her legs and dragged her deep into the woods. I tossed the rope over a tree and pulled it all the way up and tied it. She now hung upside down swinging and staring at me.

"Motherfucker, you think this is over don't you? You think this hadn't already been planned. I planned this from day one, even this moment. You are the devil Ice. You don't even know what you did."

"Shut up! Shut up, I am not the devil."

"Yes you are Michael? When I gave birth, you had a twin. You two were a gift from the devil and the Colonel helped me raise y'all. The other one was a female. I kept her hidden in the cottage in the woods away from all of y'all and taught her all of my ways. She was a better student than you and Doc, more evil and more conning. She was stronger, smarter and didn't hesitate to kill and you just helped formulate the plan by sending her into the world." Sylvia said while grinning.

I wondered what the fuck she was rambling about and how could she be grinning when she's hanging upside down. I have my machete out about to end her life. I tried and tried to figure it out but couldn't. She grinned more when she saw the confused look on my face.

"Javasia is your sister. You just gave the world a perfect offspring when you got her pregnant. It was all a plan. The devil told me to do it," she said.

I dropped my machete. I couldn't believe what the fuck I was hearing.

"Javasia is my sister?" I asked. My mind started to wonder and piece things together. She looked just like my mother and has her strength. Our bond was so powerful. "It can't be true!" I screamed.

"Yes, you stupid bastard and you fell for it."

I cried hysterically and stopped; no more crying. I left Sylvia hanging there and went back to the Colonel and grabbed his guns and holsters. "You won't need these," I mumbled then walked backed to the woods and aimed a gun at Sylvia.

BOOM! The gun roared as the first bullet tore through her stomach and came out of her back.

"Ahhh, uggghh!" she yelled in pain.

I smiled and I squeezed the trigger again and boom! I aimed for her leg shooting it off, now she's hanging from one leg. I put the gun back into the holster and picked up my machete.

"Is this what you wanted? You created this. I will be the devil that you wanted me to be. I will hate women and never trust anybody," I said through clinched teeth. I swung and the machete got stuck in her neck.

"Ugghh," she made a noise trying to breath.

I snatched the machete out of her neck and swung over and again until her head fell to the ground. I picked up her head and walked deeper into the woods knowing my destination.

"I will be heading to New York next to kill Javasia," I said out loud.

Chapter 14

In an old building in the Bronx, owned by Black Ice he had put in one of his crack-heads name, Tanya rubs her stomach while holding Tiffany's baby. Months have passed since Black Ice had moved her into this new place and still kept her cut off from the world. She looks at the two scientists, just like Black Ice had ordered her to do.

Three months ago;

"Tanya it's time." Dr. Raym said as they pressed a button, releasing all the water out of a clear tank.

Tanya stood up out her chair and walks over to them and smiles as they stared at a naked man with tubes in his body and a scar on his face. His body was pure muscles.

He opens his eyes and laughs.

"Hahahaha!" His laughter sent chills down the two scientist spines.

"Lord what have we done?" Dr. Raym mumbled.

Tanya got wet from the fear she felt and couldn't wait to have the man inside her. She looked at Tiffany's baby in her arms.

"Daddy's home," she said with a Kool-Aid smile on her face.

Chapter 15

Lawana finally felt safe in her new home in Los Angeles. Michael had helped her get as far away as she wanted from New York City. The farther she got the better she felt. She lay in her bed, in her room rubbing her stomach with the lights on. She was scared to sleep with the lights off. She closed her eyes for a second and dozed off. When she reopened them all of the lights were off. Her room door was open when she remembered closing it. She jumped up as she saw a pair of eyes staring at her from her doorway. She reached under her pillow for her gun.

"I miss you my beautiful bitch," she heard a voice whisper.

Her eyes widened as her body

trembled in fear. She fired into the darkness at the eyes that were watching her.

"It can't be! You're dead! You're dead! We killed you!" she screamed at the top of her lungs as she heard a clicking sound letting her know that her gun had been emptied.

"Ahhhh! God no! Ahhhh!" she screamed as a strong pair of hands grabbed her ankles and pulled her off of the bed and into the darkness.

"We killed you! You're dead! It can't be!

Lawana moaned in pain, her head felt like she had been hit with a sledgehammer. The last thing she remembered was Black Ice coming out of the dark in the hallway of her house and grabbing her, and then she opened her eyes for a quick second and noticed she had been thrown in a black van. Driving down the streets she noticed a dog as big as her standing next to her bleeding from the side.

Once she woke up completely she saw that she was no longer in a van but in a room with a king size bed. Her heart raced because it resembled the room she was trapped in in the warehouse of the coca cola factory. She wanted to cry as she looked down at her stomach. A familiar face came out of the room.

"Tanya that's you?" she said.

The little girl that she met a few months ago changed her hair and was much crazier. She had lost so much weight from smoking crack and she had a deranged look in her eyes.

"Yes it's me. I see he brought your ass back. I don't know why because all he need is me. But I guess he wants the child inside you," Tanya said.

Lawana stared at her funny and for the first time noticed that she was carrying a baby. Her body looked as if she could barely hold up the stomach.

I'm going to give him what he wants. He doesn't want you," Tanya stated.

"What's wrong with you girl, how did I get here? I was in LA. Where am I?"

"You're back in New York," Tanya said as she lay down on the bed.

"What do you mean give him what he wants; I thought Black Ice was dead. How the fuck did I end up here? It's no way he can be alive." Lawana said as she cried hysterically.

"That's where you're wrong. My man can't die," Tanya said.

"Your man?"

"Yes bitch, my man." Tanya said. She pulled a knife out of nowhere and stabbed Lawana in the stomach.

"Ahhh, what are you doing?" Lawana cried out.

Tanya skid the knife across the lower part of her stomach, opening her up to see two pair of legs.

"This all he wanted bitch, the twins," Tanya said as she grabbed one of the babies and pulled it out.

'Waaaah!' the baby cried as she cut the umbilical cord.

"Ahhhh, ugghh!" Lawana screamed.

She tried to fight as Tanya reached in and removed the other baby cutting the umbilical cord.

"He's mine bitch and you can never have him." Tanya said as she raised the knife high.

A sound caught her attention before she came down with the knife. She turned around to see Black Ice standing in the doorway. Black Ice stared at her covered in blood then stared at Lawana.

"Bitch, what are you doing?" Black Ice hollered.

"Nothing," Tanya said as she dropped the knife.

Chapter 16

Michael Jr. stood up and couldn't believe what he was reading. He wiped his eyes. "What the fuck?" he said out loud as he stared at the jars with Sylvia and his father's head in them. "My fucking family is twisted, this can't be true. What the hell?" Michael Jr. said to himself. He started to close the book but something told him to turn to the next page. His phone was vibrating. He checked it and saw that it was a text from his mother.

'Boy I told you not to ignore me, the devil is not dead, he's real, and he's still alive. Keep your eyes open,' the text read. He put the phone back into his pocket and turned the page of the thick book and his mouth opened up wide in shock as he saw

his name, 'Evil', the name people call him on the streets.

Evil, my son, I knew you would be the only one to find this book. It has plenty of stories in it. You also need to know that the same blood that runs through Sylvia runs through all of us, so you can't fight who you are. You are just like us, but know this; I will be coming back for Mike. I have more kids out there; you have a sister named Shanelle, who's part Trinidadian, hiding out in New York. You also have a nephew; Wanno, who's an offspring of your deceased brother Noble. There's a Detective Alexis Lovett, she had a son that wasn't evil enough and he died but left an offspring; a beautiful daughter named Shenice, I will be grabbing her. I have

two more sons that are great killers but too soft. Their names are Bless and Damou. Bless has picked the perfect wife, Tess; who happens to be an assassin. Tess met and fell in love with Iris. They both are professional killers and have two daughters named Isis and Ayoyna and they have great potential. I will teach them to be great killers and help rid the weak and dominate the world. I will be coming for them. So I will see you soon. You know where to find me, deep in the woods in North Carolina.

Michael Jr. couldn't believe what he was reading, "I have more siblings and some of them are my age, what the fuck? Thank God it's over. Thank God I killed him so he will never be able to touch my kids or my sibling's kids ever."

"Hahaha, that's what you think."

Michael Jr. jumped as he heard the voice echo. He grabbed his machete and looked out of the trophy room and couldn't believe his eyes. It was his father but not as he was before. He looked younger and much stronger. He had a machete in his hand and was wearing nothing but a tank top and a long leather jacket. Michael Jr. trembled in fear as he looked back and forth from his father's head in the jar to the look-alike standing before him.

"This can't be you're dead; you're dead!" Michael screamed.

"You can't kill the devil," Black Ice said. I'm coming for all my children Michael. Either you follow my in footsteps or die with the rest."

"Never!" Michael screamed as he charged at Black Ice with the machete as all the lights in the house went out. Michael studied the room for movement and in seconds the lights came back on and Black Ice was gone.

"THIS CAN'T BE REAL! I must've imagined it reading that fucking journal!" Michael screamed as his phone vibrated in his pocket. He grabbed it and saw that it was another text from his mother and read it.

'The devil is near you. Be ready!'

Made in the USA
Monee, IL
25 January 2025

10958066R00152